P. M. Hubbard and The Murder Room

>>> This title is part of The Murder Room, our series dedicated to making available out-of-print or hard-to-find titles by classic crime writers.

Crime fiction has always held up a mirror to society. The Victorians were fascinated by sensational murder and the emerging science of detection; now we are obsessed with the forensic detail of violent death. And no other genre has so captivated and enthralled readers.

Vast troves of classic crime writing have for a long time been unavailable to all but the most dedicated frequenters of second-hand bookshops. The advent of digital publishing means that we are now able to bring you the backlists of a huge range of titles by classic and contemporary crime writers, some of which have been out of print for decades.

From the genteel amateur private eyes of the Golden Age and the femmes fatales of pulp fiction, to the morally ambiguous hard-boiled detectives of mid twentieth-century America and their descendants who walk our twenty-first century streets, The Murder Room has it all. >>>

The Murder Room
Where Criminal Minds Meet

themurderroom.com

T0352157

P. M. Hubbard (1910–1980)

Praised by critics for his clean prose style, characterization, and the strong sense of place in his novels, Philip Maitland Hubbard was born in Reading, in Berkshire and brought up in Guernsey, in the Channel Islands. He was educated at Oxford, where he won the Newdigate Prize for English verse in 1933. From 1934 until its disbandment in 1947 he served with the Indian Civil Service. On his return to England he worked for the British Council, eventually retiring to work as a freelance writer. He contributed to a number of publications, including *Punch*, and wrote 16 novels for adults as well as two children's books. He lived in Dorset and Scotland, and many of his novels draw on his interest in and knowledge of rural pursuits and folk religion.

The Causeway

P. M. Hubbard

An Orion book

Copyright © Caroline Dumonteil, Owain Rhys Phillips and Maria
Marcela Appleby Gomez 1969, 2012

The right of P. M. Hubbard to be identified as the author of this work
has been asserted in accordance with the Copyright, Designs and Patents
Act 1988.

This edition published by
The Orion Publishing Group Ltd
Orion House
5 Upper St Martin's Lane
London WC2H 9EA

An Hachette UK company
A CIP catalogue record for this book is available from the British Library

ISBN 978 1 4719 0061 7

www.orionbooks.co.uk

Chapter One

I am no more than a small-boat sailor at best, and do not reckon to blind anyone with nautical technicalities. But if I say that I lost my rudder a hundred yards off a lee shore, most people will understand that it meant trouble. A rudder, they will surely know, is what you steer a boat with, and a lee shore, they will probably remember, is a shore with the wind blowing on to it. If you cannot steer your boat, it will just get pushed along in the direction the wind is blowing, and if the wind is blowing on shore, it will get pushed on shore. That is what happened to me that Saturday afternoon early in September.

There was no danger to me in the thing, or not in any way I could anticipate then. It was a mild day with a moderate breeze from the south. In these rather shallow waters even a moderate breeze can raise a short, steep little sea, which may break even before it comes ashore, but so far as I myself was concerned, I could have gone overboard there and then and swum ashore without the least difficulty. It was the boat I was worried about. It was a good solid old wooden boat. I was very fond of it, and if I had lost it, I should have been hard put to it to get another anything like it at current prices. If it had been driven on to rocks, with that sea and the tide still making,

1

it would have been in real danger of breaking up altogether, and even if I had gone ashore with it, there would have been very little I could do. A beach would be a different matter, but from where I was I could not see any beach, only a steep-to shore with black up-ended rocks under it and that short, rolling sea breaking among them.

And the trouble was, I did not know where I was, or not in any detail. I know that sounds nonsense. You do not sail uncharted seas in a fourteen-foot sailing dinghy. Of course I knew where I was to a mile or so on the map. I was sailing from Vance Bay, where I had my moorings, round to Canty Port, where I was going to spend the night with the Marlings. I was not navigating, I was just sailing by sight, as you walk across country from one place to another. There would be no mistaking Canty Port when I came to it, and in these conditions the thing was just a pleasure trip with a mild spice of adventure in it. It feels good arriving anywhere by sea.

But I was new to these parts, and did not know much about the coastline in between. I had reckoned to stay clear of it until I started to make in towards the Port. But I was going so well, sailing smoothly across that steady southerly breeze, that I edged in a bit close round what looked like a small bare headland and it was just there that the thing happened. Not that a hundred yards is very close by small-boat standards, but it was close enough to call for pretty quick action, and I was not at all sure what action I could take.

The boat of course turned up into the wind and hung there, yawing about with the sails flapping in that rolling sea, while I tried to see what the trouble was. I had not lost the rudder altogether. It was still there on the end of the tiller, which came in through a slot in the top of the

2

transom, but it was no longer fixed to the boat. It had nothing to swivel on, and was as useless and awkward as a door off its hinges. From what I could see in those few hectic seconds, the top eye had carried away, and the pintle, which is the vertical pin the bottom of the rudder swivels on, had slewed over sideways. At any rate, I could see there was no possibility of getting the rudder back into proper use, and when I looked up again, I was already perceptibly nearer to the rocks.

Once I had made sure that the rudder could not carry away altogether, I left the tiller and went forward and got the mainsail down. I got it down in any sort of order along the middle of the boat. This took the wind pressure off and cut down our rate of drift to leeward. I left the foresail as it was, with enough sheet to sail across the wind. With a good rudder, you can make surprising progress on the foresail alone. The question was whether I could somehow get enough work out of the rudder, as it was, to make the boat pay off again and go across the wind at least until I could see somewhere where there was a chance of getting her ashore without too much damage. She was going ashore sooner or later whatever I did. The best I could hope for was some choice of where she did it.

I took the tiller in one hand and leaned over the transom and got hold of the top of the rudder with the other. I flapped it in the water until the boat's head came round and the wind came into the starboard side of the sail. Then I wrestled wildly to hold her off the wind, and we began to creep eastwards again. My right side was strained across the top of the transom, and my right arm, at full stretch downwards, took all the pull of the wind on the boat. The rolling made it worse. It was desperate work, and I did not know how long I could keep it up. At times we seemed to be holding a good line, and I thought we should clear the point, though I could not tell how far the rocks ran out under water. At others we seemed to make more leeway than headway, and I thought we had no chance at all. What there was on the other side of the point I did not know, but at least, if it was a point, there must be more searoom to leeward. That was the limit of my ambition.

The bottom had begun shelving up under us, and the seas were getting steeper. It was not only the wind that was pushing the boat ashore now, it was the water itself, and all the time she was getting more and more difficult to handle. We were dead to windward of the point, and not more than thirty yards out, when a violent roll broke the resistance of my weakening muscles, and she came right up into the wind again, pitching now instead of rolling, and drifting steadily stern-first on to the black rocks. It is curious, looking back, to remember the depth of my desperation at that moment, when I was, I repeat, in no sort of danger myself at all. There were times later when I quite certainly was, and I am sure I never experienced the same panic. I suppose the small-boat sailor, no less than the captain of a ship, identifies himself with his craft as you do with no other means of transport, except perhaps a small boy with his first bicycle and a few grown men I have known with their cars.

I wrenched at that damned rudder and got her head round for the last time, and just as she started to edge forward across the wind again, I looked up and saw salvation ahead. The rocks broke off suddenly in a sort of small cliff, and beyond it, between that and another sloping saw-edge of black rock, there was a narrow inlet running in to a shingle beach. I held her, somehow, until I thought the rocks were no longer under our lee, and then

4

I let the rudder go and scrambled to get the centre-plate up before it caught the bottom and turned us over in the surf.

Everything happened very quickly after that. The sea took hold of us and we slewed broadside on to it. She bumped once, not too hard, on what must have been a mercifully rounded rock under water, and then, with only yards to spare between our bows and stern and the rocks on either side, we rolled sideways on to the beach. I jumped out into waist-high water, nearly lost my footing when the boat tried to roll on top of me, got my balance again just in time, grabbed the transom with its dangling useless rudder and pulled her stern-first on to the shingle. I was calm again now. I stood there with the water washing round my knees, and as each successive wave lifted her, I threw all my weight back and dragged her a little further up the beach. She was out of danger now. She must have lost a bit of paint off her bottom, but that was the limit of the damage. I pulled my sodden guernsey sleeve back from my wrist and looked at my watch. It was full high water. In that respect at least the thing could not have timed itself better. I had only to hold her steady for a bit against the odd bigger wave, and the sea would leave her, comfortably beached at the head of the tiny bay. Disaster had been averted, and for the moment all was well. Only I still had not the faintest idea where I was.

I suppose it was that that turned my mind to the next stage of what I had to do, and, with no wave immediately threatening the boat, I turned for a moment, still holding the transom with both hands, and looked over my shoulder inland. The rocks which formed the sides of the little bay ran back in high ridges under turf and heather, but between them, at the top of the beach, a narrow cleft

5

climbed less steeply to the bare skyline. There were no trees to speak of, but the cleft was blocked from side to side with a dense thorn scrub, with what looked like an animal track wandering through it. Then a wave caught the boat and heaved the bow up, and I turned quickly to steady her. It was just as I turned that I saw what I thought was a man watching me. It was only a head and shoulders on the skyline, a bit off to one side, and I saw it only out of the corner of my eye as I turned, but I did not think I could have been mistaken. For all my comparative calm, a great sense of relief welled up in me. I had, after all, to get help of one sort or another, and to find help so close at hand was another big step forward out of my predicament. I concentrated on the boat for a moment or two, and then turned round again to make sure of him, but he was no longer there.

I thought perhaps he was already on his way down towards me, and I spent some time holding the boat, with the occasional glance over my shoulder, expecting him at any moment to hail me from somewhere near at hand. When he did not, I began to wonder whether perhaps he had been too much of a landsman to understand the position I was in. So far from being a friendly helper, he might be the local owner, resentful of what he would see as a wanton and unwelcome intrusion on his property. In either case I wanted to speak to him. It was not till some time later that I began to wonder whether he really had been there at all. I tried looking over my shoulder at the place where I thought I had seen him, but I could see nothing there which I could, in whatever state of confusion, have mistaken for a man's head and shoulders. I could not really believe I had imagined him. I thought he had been there, and had seen me, and had gone away again without making contact. I could not see why he should have done that, but I thought perhaps in due course I should find out.

The sea had nearly left the boat now, and I had time to see in detail what had happened. The pintle, which had been screwed on to the transom, had pulled out two of its three screws and swung sideways, releasing the eye of the rudder which swivelled on it. With its bottom freed, the whole rudder had then swung sideways too, wrenching the top eye out of the transom altogether. I still had the pintle, hanging on by its one remaining screw, and this was lucky, because it would not be easy to replace, and even a temporary substitute would be extraordinarily hard to improvise. The top eye on the transom, in which the pin of the rudder had engaged, was missing altogether. No doubt it was on the mud a hundred yards out from the end of the rocks, but I did not think the tide would go out that far, even in these shoal waters, and even if it did, the chance of finding the thing was remote. But a substitute of some sort, good enough to get me back on to my moorings, should not be too difficult. Even a large eye-bolt might do it. If I could get to an iron-monger's, or even a farm workshop in these mechanical days, I thought I could make a job of the boat where she was on the beach.

The sea was still washing round the bows occasionally, but it would not shift the boat now. I could not remember whether the next flood would be bigger or smaller, but in any case I had twelve hours to do what I had to do and get back to the boat before it happened. It was time I tidied up, and put on some dry trousers, and started my exploration.

I got the sails down and properly stowed, and made all secure on board. Then I got my land trousers and a pair of leather shoes out of my kitbag in the bows. It was a comfort to think that I had been ship-wrecked on the only occasion, so far as I could remember, when I had ever had a change of clothes on board. I hung the wet trousers and my ropesoles on a thorn-bush to dry as best they could, but the sun was off the beach already, and I did not think they would dry very quickly. Finally I got out a length of spare line and made one end fast round the centre thwart. I carried the other end over the transom and up the beach, and made it fast round the roots of the biggest thorn-bush I could find. It takes an enormous amount of horizontal drag to shift the roots of even a good-sized bush, and there was nothing else to make it fast to. Even if I failed to get back before the next high water, I did not think the boat could take much harm now, or not unless the wind freshened a lot and stayed southerly, and that seemed a very unlikely combination.

By now it was past five o'clock, and from where I was the sun was over the western skyline. There was plenty of daylight left, but the September evenings are short in these parts, and it was time I got moving. I looked over everything, could think of nothing more I ought to do, and set out up the track. It was tricky and a little painful, but perfectly negotiable. As I came out on to the turf slope above the thorn, the tops of the inland hills came up over the skyline ahead of me. They did not look more than a mile or two away, and the farms would be on their lower slopes. I should not have very far to go. The next thing I saw was the chimneys of a house, just over the skyline and not more than a couple of hundred yards ahead. That was even better, though I wondered if that was where my watcher had come from, and if so, what sort of reception I should meet when I got there. Anyhow, there was only one way of finding out. I hurried up the last of the slope, came out over the top of the ridge and stopped dead in my tracks.

There was the house, a solid looking stone building only a short walk ahead. There were the inland hills, with at least one good-sized house less than a quarter of a mile away. But between them, shining white under the late afternoon sky, a sheet of water, all of two hundred yards wide, stretched right across my front and curved round east and west on either hand. Unmistakably, it was sea water, rolling steadily in the southerly breeze. I knew then what I had done. It was not a headland I had come ashore on. It was an off-shore island. They happen, of course, on this very broken coast, but I had not known there was one between Vance Bay and Canty Port. The land came round it on both sides, and it had not looked like an island from out at sea, or at least not from the angle I had come in on. But there it was. Welcome or unwelcome, I had only the one house to go to.

The ground fell away in front of me now. The house was on the inshore slope of the island. I went on towards it, and the nearer I got, the less I liked the look of it. There were only a few small outbuildings round it, and no signs of life or any recognisable farming activity. As far as I could see in any direction, there was no land under plough. It was all rough turf broken by the occasional dry-stone wall. Sheep-run possibly, but not farm land. I walked on, cautiously now, as though something was lying in wait for me, though I did not know what it might be. It was only as I came up to the house that I saw the ground-floor windows staring blankly at me like blind eyes. They were shuttered on the inside. The wind blew over the bare turf and the grey stone, and nothing moved. I could not argue the thing any longer. The house was empty.

Chapter Two

I went on, of course. For one thing, I had to make sure, and for another, I had nowhere else to go. I walked all round the house, peering at everything and even trying the odd door, as though I could somehow break down its resistance by refusing to take no for an answer. It was not a ruin, or even, in the usual sense of the word, derelict. It was clearly not in use, but it was, as they say of land, in hand. There were no slates missing from the roof and no panes missing from the windows. The doors needed paint, but they were in good condition and firmly locked. One or two of the outhouses had doors on the bolt, but there was nothing inside them. The house was on two floors, with perhaps three rooms on each floor. All the ground-floor windows were shuttered on the inside, and the shutters were closed. You could not see into the house at all. The first-floor windows were of course out of reach. From what I could see, I did not think they were shuttered and indeed they would not be in these parts, but they were all closed. It occurred to me that if I went back to the higher ground, I might be able to see whether they had curtains, but the point was not of much importance at the moment. It might just possibly be someone's holiday house—it would be a marvellous place for one, if you had a boat and like solitude—though if it was, the owner did not seem to be giving it more than the minimal upkeep. But it was not, at the moment, lived in. My momentary watcher must have been imaginary, unless he was lurking somewhere about the island, and that did not make much sense. My only hope was the mainland, in particular the house I could see just on the other side of the water. I might be able to attract their attention in some way. If the worse came to the worst, I could swim for it, but I was not going to try that yet.

For the moment my position was in no sense desperate. I had brought sandwiches and a flask of tea for the trip, and had not yet started on them when the disaster occurred. There must be fresh water somewhere, or the house would not be there. Probably there would be a well, but it would not be an open well nowadays. It would be sealed, and the water piped into the house. There would be a diesel pump, or perhaps, if they wanted electricity, a diesel generator and an electric pump for the water. But I was not going to die of thirst either, or certainly not before I could swim to the mainland. I decided to try signalling for help while the daylight lasted. If that did no good, I would sleep where I was and do my swim in the morning. It was only when I came to consider signalling as a practical proposition that I realised the difficulties I was up against.

The most effective form of signal in a place like that is fire, to make smoke by day and show a light by night. But I had no means of lighting a fire. I do not smoke and therefore carry no lighter or matches. There were these stories of people using their spectacle lenses as a burning glass, but I do not wear glasses either, and in any case the sun no longer had that sort of power in it. I had no kind of a torch with me. All I could think of was movement.

There was nothing to hoist an improvised flag on, but I could get up on to the most conspicuous place and wave some sort of flag by hand in the hope that someone would notice it. It was exasperatingly chancy, but I did not see what else I could do.

That raised the question of what to use for a flag. In the comic drawings of shipwrecked mariners and desert-islands castaways the man has always tied the two sleeves of his shirt to the mast and the shirt is blowing out bravely, but I do not know if the people who do these drawings have ever tried this for themselves, or even seen it done. In fact there is much less tying length in the ordinary shirtsleeve than the drawings suggest. I know, because I tried it later. In any case, I did not want to take my shirt off. Even with two sets of clothes available, at least for my top half, I knew I was going to be cold before the night was out, and I was not going to risk getting cold now. The only thing I could think of was the foresail of the boat. A fourteen-foot dinghy has a small triangular foresail, generally with the sheets permanently attached to it. It should be possible to make a flag of it, and I could use the boat-hook, or even the main boom, for a pole. At least it was worth trying.

I made my way back to the boat again. I should have liked to walk round the island, but there was no time for that. As far as I could see, it could not be more than three hundred yards across in any direction. Whether there were any other beaches I did not know. If there were, they were probably on the landward side. I got the foresail out of the bag and saw at once that the boat-hook was much too short for the job. The main boom was too long and too solid to be handled easily, but there was nothing else. By the time I had got the sheet off it and carried it back to the top of the island, with the foresail bundled

12

under it on my shoulder, I was dismayed to find how fast
the light was going. I took the gear up to the highest
point, which was south-west of the house, tied the sail not
very convincingly to one end of the boom, put the other
end on the turf and began to wave the thing from side to
side, watching the house on the mainland for any sort of
response, or indeed for any sign of life. I felt not very
hopeful and extraordinarily foolish. To say I felt conspicuous sounds silly, because to be conspicuous was the ob-
ject of the whole manoeuvre, but conspicuous is what I
felt. I suppose the truth is that although I had to make
my predicament known to someone, I did not like admit-
ting it in that very public and amateurish way. I felt I
was behaving like a week-end tripper adrift in a hired
boat, and even with my limited seamanship I did not like
it.

Also, it was unexpectedly tiring, and I found I could
not keep it up indefinitely, but had to rest between spells
of my idiotic waving. At least it kept me warm, but I
could no longer disguise from myself the fact that I was
very hungry and, what was worse, thirsty. I kept at it
until I could see less and less detail on the land opposite,
and all the time I saw nothing stir at the house I was
watching and, even when it was getting towards dark, no
lights. I began to wonder whether that too was empty.
The chances were that the island went with the land attached to the house, and I supposed it was possible that
the whole place was unoccupied, though it did not seem
likely. The wind had gone completely now, and a sea mist
began to creep in over the water between me and the
land. So far as the boat was concerned, this was all to the
good, but it just about put paid to my chances of being
seen. I do not know how long I kept at it altogether, but
finally I gave it up and began thinking about food and

sleep. I took the sail off the boom. I was not going to waste time signalling again in the morning. If I was going to have to swim, I intended to do it before hunger took too much of the stuffing out of me. I put the gear on my shoulder again and walked back down to the house.

It looked extraordinarily forbidding in the grey dusk, and when I came to it, I did not like the feel of the place at all. The obvious thing, with the mist coming up and possibly even rain later, was to bed down somehow in one of the outhouses, but I could not bring myself to do it. I told myself that I had to be near the boat when the tide came up a little before dawn, but with a dead calm sea I did not really believe that there would be anything for me to do when it did. The truth is that I wanted to get away from the house. I gave one last look at the land opposite. I could see points of light now, but all much further back on the lower slopes of the hills. I heaved the boom on my shoulder again and set off back to the boat.

I looked everything over in the half light, but there was nothing new to see and nothing that needed doing. The sea was well clear of the boat now, dropping very slowly down the small, steep beach. There was no wind at all, and the water barely lapped on the pebbles. That was the only sound I could hear. The curve of the island stood dark above me, but out to sea my vision tailed off, I could not tell at what distance, into the luminous opacity of the sea mist. Overhead the sky was clear, with the bigger stars already beginning to show.

I put the boom back into the boat and made it fast. The foresail I kept out. I had the idea that it might serve me, one way or another, as bedding. I got the pullover and jacket belonging to my shore clothes out of the bag and put them on, the pullover under my guernsey and the jacket over it. Then at last I got the bag of provisions and

14

let myself eat and drink. The tea was still hot and went
down marvellously. I left the last cupful in the flask. It
would get cold overnight, but stay wet. I also left one of
the sandwiches. I did not like leaving either, but I had
the morning to think of. I then set about finding somewhere to sleep. It was obviously impossible to get comfortable on the beach. You can sleep on sand, but not on
pebbles, or not unless they are very small and rounded. I
decided that the best place was on one of the small ridges
that flanked the bay. There was turf and heather up
there, and the lying ought to be reasonably soft, given a
bit of preparation. I climbed up the sea bank and did
what I could. The solution I finally came up with was to
spread the foresail, which was thick nylon, over a mattress of heather. I took the heather as it grew, with a few
up-rooted bushes to fill in the obvious gaps. I lay down
with my head on the peak of the sail, and used the width
at the bottom to turn a flap over my legs, which were less
well covered than the rest of me. I lay on my back, looking up at the stars, with the silence all round me and the
sea mist closing in.

To lie out in the heather under the stars is supposed to
have been a rewarding experience for half the heroes of
Scotland, fictional and historical, but I cannot say I took
to it. Even with the thick sail over it, the heather did not
seem to make very comfortable lying. It was certainly
springy, but the springiness was irregular, pushing up
parts of my body that I wanted down and letting down
parts that wanted support. I arranged myself as best I
could, but the result remained unsatisfactory. Then, just
as I had resigned myself to wakefulness, I went to sleep.
What is more, I must have slept quite deeply, because I
woke out of a dream, and took some time to sort out the
dream from reality.

15

I forget the circumstances of my dream, but there was someone shouting in it. I woke up, wondered for a moment where I was and then remembered. I felt cold and a little damp, but did not sit up. I was trying to remember the dream, and why someone in it had been shouting to me, when suddenly, quite close at hand, someone shouted again. It was a man's voice. It said, "A-hooy! Anyone there?" It had the long-drawn penetrant quality of a naval hail, and the accent was unmistakably English, not Scots. I struggled up into a sitting position, cleared the cold mucus from the back of my throat and shouted back.

I shouted, "Ahoy! Dinghy on the beach." I said that because I thought that the man, whoever he was, would probably know where the beach was. A moment later a light came on, and a beam shone out from the opposite ridge, dipped to the boat for a moment and then lifted and settled on me as I sat clasping my knees on the foresail. For the second time that evening I felt uncommonly foolish. Of all things in the world, I wished I cut a more seamanlike figure (it must have been something in the man's voice), but with a tweed jacket on my top half and the bottom of the sail wrapped round my legs I could not look anything but a pretty foolish virgin. All this time the light held steady on me. It was a blindingly powerful beam, and I could not see at all what was behind it. For a disconcertingly long time the owner of the voice considered me in silence from behind his light. Then he said, "What are you doing here?"

It was a perfectly straightforward question. There were no overtones in it at all. He just wanted to know, and I assumed, as in the circumstances I must, that he had a right to. I had a perfectly good explanation, only I wished he would take that damned light off me, and let me disentangle myself from the sail and stand up in relative privacy. As he did not, I sat where I was, looking at him sideways. I said, "I lost my rudder out to windward. I had to beach her."

Only then the light dipped to the boat again, and I seized the opportunity to struggle to my feet. With the light no longer in my eyes, I could just see a single figure standing opposite me across the narrow beach. It looked a big figure, but I could not see any detail. Then the light was turned on me again. He said, "You've still got your rudder."

I had, of course, and thank God for it. It was still hanging by the tiller on the transom. By torchlight and at that distance it looked all right. I suddenly got angry. I did not like being interrogated under a spotlight, as if I was a man assisting the police with their enquiries. I said, "I didn't say it had carried away. I lost the use of it. I'll show you." I started to scramble down the bank on to the beach, but I still had the light in my eyes, and I missed my footing and came down in an undignified slither that did not make me feel any better. Once on the beach, I walked down to the boat without further mishap. I took hold of the rudder and pulled it away from the transom, with the tiller running out through its slot at the top. The light had followed me, and now I felt more like a conjurer showing the audience that there has been no deception.

"I see," he said. "Where did this happen?"

"About a hundred yards out and about a hundred westwards."

There was a moment's silence. Then he said, "You did well to get her in."

My anger vanished abruptly. I felt I had been judged by my peer, to put it no higher, and my action approved. "I was lucky," I said. "I thought I was going on the rocks, but I opened the beach just in time."

17

He said again, "I see," and with my new-found morale I asked him what I myself, not unnaturally, wanted to know.

"For the matter of that," I said, "how did you get here?"

"Oh," he said, "I walked."

"From where?"

"From the land. The island's only tidal. But you want to know the way."

I felt suddenly very foolish again. With the soundings as they are round here, I should have thought of that instead of carrying on like Robinson Crusoe. He must have felt he had the advantage of me, because he went back to his enquiry. He said, "Where are you from, then?"

Once more the question had no overtones, and it was a natural one in the circumstances. "The other side of Vance Bay," I said. "I was making for Canty Port."

"I see." He paused for a moment, as if he was considering the whole situation. "Well," he said, "what can I do for you?"

I said, "Take that damned light out of my eyes for a start," and he laughed. It was quite a pleasant laugh, but very self-assured.

"Sorry," he said. "I didn't realise I was blinding you." He turned the beam on to the ground at his feet, and then, with the light to guide him, scrambled down his side and joined me on the beach. He said, "What else do you need?"

He was a big man, a good head taller than I was and I judged a good many years older. He had his hair cut very short, or else was slightly bald. The face was squarish, but I could not see much of the features. The light showed more of the bottom half of him, and I saw he was wearing waders. "I shall need some bits and pieces for repairs," I

18

said. "Then I reckon I can get her off again. Tomorrow
will do for that, of course. For the moment, to be honest,
I could do with something to eat and drink." I thought for
a moment. "Oh," I said, "and if possible I'd like to get
word to my friends at Canty Port, or they'll be alerting
the coastguards."

Once more he considered the whole situation. "I tell
you what," he said. "I suggest you come back with me.
We'll feed you and give you a bed for the night. And you
can telephone your friends. It's not very late yet. Then in
the morning you can see what you need to get afloat
again."

"That's very kind of you," I said. "I'd be enormously
grateful, of course."

"That's all right," he said. "But we'd better get moving.
The tide will be over the causeway in another half-hour.
Anything you want from the boat?"

"Just my things," I said. I got the kitbag out of the
bows. Then I remembered my wet things. I took them
off their thorn-bush. They were damp but no longer really
wet, and I stuffed them into the top of the bag. I was
anxious to appear ready and able. I swung the bag over
my shoulder. "Ready," I said.

He said, "Good. I'll go ahead with the light." He
turned and started up the track, and I followed him.

19

Chapter Three

It is not only hindsight that makes me say that that was an extraordinary walk. I really felt it at the time. I was not afraid—I had nothing to be afraid of—but I deliberately surrendered myself to the totally unknown. When you have been thrown into a strange man's company by pure chance, and the two of you have embarked on a course of action together, there is a compelling human instinct to learn a little more about each other. That is, unless the course of action is one which occupies your entire attention, and now we were only walking, one behind the other. But we walked in total silence. I thought the mist had cleared a bit, as it often does a little later in the night, when the day's warmth has gone out of land and water. But I could not really tell. The sky overhead was full of stars, but there was no moon. I could see very little round me, and in any case I was concerned mainly to watch the circle of torchlight ahead and the figure that walked steadily on between me and it.

We walked up over the hump of the island and down the other side. I could see no lights anywhere on the mainland, and yet it was barely eleven o'clock. There must be more mist still than I had thought. I never saw the house on the island. I thought we had at some point jinked to the right off my line of the afternoon, and on a hump like that quite a short distance unsights you. Presently we were going steeply downhill again, though the track was straighter and there were turf banks on either side. I could smell the mud now. There is not much firm sand anywhere on this coast, or not exposed to the air. The silt that comes down the rivers and washes off the low shores covers it, and for all our perpetual winds and breaking seas, we hardly ever get the full force of the Atlantic rollers to scour it clean. Then there was shingle under our feet, and for the first time the man stopped and spoke. He said, "Better take your shoes off, I think, and roll your trousers up a couple of turns. It's a bit soft, but no more than ankle-deep if you follow me closely."

I took the leather shoes off and knotted the laces and hung them round my neck. I was wearing no socks. He kept the light on the ground while I did it. Then he said, "Right. Off we go, then. Don't get off the line if you can help it."

I nodded, though he probably could not see it. I did not want to say anything. He turned and went on again, and I went after him, treading in his steps like the page behind Good King Wenceslas. For all his extra height, his stride was no longer than mine. But then you do not stride out in waders. And he was right about the mud. It seemed only a few inches over firm going, and if I stepped right in his footmarks, I hardly felt it, though I could smell it all the time. We marched out like that, stepping in perfect time, into the middle of nowhere. We did not at any point seem to alter course abruptly, but I thought we were moving in a steady curve. There was nothing to mark the line, but he must have known it very accurately. I could see nothing but almost flat mud in every direction, but then I could not see more than a yard or two in any detail. I was conscious only of a faintly shimmering waste all round us and the salt, sour smell everywhere. There was not a breath of wind, and no sound at all but the steady squelching of our feet. I do not think I have ever been so completely in another man's power, but there was nothing in it to worry me, even if I had felt inclined to worry. I could not say at all how long we walked like that. It cannot really have been very long. Then I saw darkness ahead and on both sides of us, and in another minute we were on shingle again.

He stopped and said, "Better put your shoes on now. They'll get a bit messy, but it'll wash off. It isn't far now."

For the second time I did what I was told without saying anything, and for the second time he waited while I did it, with the light of the torch in a circle round our feet. Then he turned and went on along the beach, and presently the beach turned into a made road, with trees and shrubbery growing thick on both sides.

I had assumed from the start that he came from the first house, the one overlooking the passage between the island and the mainland. I had no real reason to assume this, except the fact that he behaved like the owner of the island, and it would belong, if to anyone, to the owner of that house. Also, I did not see who else would have seen my signals, and I assumed that he must have seen them, or he would not have come looking for me. I made a lot of assumptions about him from the start, but then I had no facts to speak of, and the human mind wants some basis to work on. I was right about the house, at least. Now that I no longer needed to keep my eyes fixed on that mesmeric spot of moving light, I could look about me, and there was something now for my eyes to focus on. As a result, my night sight, which was normally good, was re-asserting itself, and I began to see quite a lot.

I could see that his hair was, in fact, cut short, at least on the back of his head, and that it was pale in colour, though whether it was blond or grey I could not yet tell. I could see that he wore a thick turtle-neck sweater, black or dark blue, with his waders braced right up over the bottom of it, and that his shoulders were very powerful, even allowing for the thickness of wool over them. He had the walk of a powerful man, too. I have never tried to define this, but mostly there is no mistaking it. And his voice, for all his easy way of using it, came out of a deep chest. Then the road passed between stone gateposts, and the bushes stopped, leaving us on a slope of open ground, with the drive, if that was what it was, climbing on a sideways slant across it. There was quite a lot of this before we came to the house, but there was no sign of a garden, or of cultivation of any sort. I thought the house must stand clear in the middle of an open space, probably with a wall round it and the natural greenery growing thick outside the wall, and I found later that this was so. When we came to the house, we came to what must be the eastern end of it, and we went along its northern side, where a stone porch stood out at the centre. It looked a typical farmhouse of the local stone, and like many such it turned its back on the sea. I wondered whether that was why I had seen no lights from the island. I could see lights now in the ground-floor windows, but all muffled behind thick curtains. The door was solid and had no transom light, and the porch itself was in darkness. When we came to it, he brought a key out of his pocket and opened what must be a latch-lock to let us in. I remember this struck me as a little odd, but I had no time to give any thought to it.

He threw open the door and then, for the first time, stood aside and ushered me in ahead of him. It was a naturally courteous gesture, but then I did not expect him to be anything but well-mannered. I walked into a long narrow hall, which I thought must run back to almost the full depth of the house. The stairs ran up one side of it. There was a door at the foot of the stairs, two doors on the other side and a door at the far end, though whether it was the back door of the house I could not tell. The hall was rather dimly lit from a single bulb in the ceiling. I had no time to take in much detail, but I knew it was not a farmer's hall. There is no mistaking that. Then the door opened on the left, and a woman came out of a more brightly lit room and stood facing us in the doorway.

The man behind me spoke for the first time since we had come on to the beach. He said, "I've brought in a ship-wrecked mariner. Can we give him a bed for the night, do you think?"

The woman said, "Of course. Come in. What happened?"

She spoke to me. I was blinking a bit in the light, but I got the impression of a pale face with dark hair and eyes. Her voice was low and wonderfully pleasant. She was as dark and slender as her husband was fair and broad. I said, "My rudder came adrift, and I had to beach the boat. It's very kind of you. I hope I'm not being a nuisance."

I knew she had been waiting to hear me speak, as you do, especially in a part of the country where there are huge variations in speech, and all of them significant. She smiled and said, "Not a bit. It's nice to have visitors. We don't see many." Her eyes went over my shoulder for a moment to her husband, and I was aware, just for that moment, of a faint suggestion of tension or challenge, but when he spoke, his voice was warm and pleasant.

24

He said, "I don't know your name. My name's Barlow. This is Letty, my wife."

"Grant," I said, "Peter. How do you do?"

She put out a hand and we shook hands solemnly. Her hand was slender, but the fingers were very strong. She said, "How do you do. Mr. Grant? Now, what can we do for you?"

Barlow said, "You want to telephone, don't you? Perhaps we'd better get that over first. It may save trouble for other people."

"If you please," I said. "I don't want the police or the coastguards looking for me."

"Of course not. And your friends will be worried if they're expecting you. Letty, will you show Mr. Grant the phone while I go and get these things off?"

She said, "Of course. In here, Mr. Grant." There was a door through into another room, and she led me into it. The room we had first come into was a sitting-room, but this was a working-room, with a desk and cupboards and books on built-in shelves. The telephone was on the desk. As we went in, Barlow went out into the hall, and in the back of my mind I heard the stairs creak as he went upstairs. They would be old stairs, and he was a heavy man. Mrs. Barlow said, "You know the number?" I nodded, and she said, "Good. Well, I'll leave you to it." She went back into the sitting-room and shut the door behind her.

I dialled the number and stood with the receiver to my ear, listening to the phone ringing at the far end. Then there was a small click on the line, and a moment later the ringing stopped and I heard Susie Marling's voice. She was a rather silly little woman, Susie, but very friendly. It was mainly Bill I went over to see. I said, "Susie? This is Pete."

25

She said, "Oh, Pete. Where are you, for God's sake? We've been so worried."

I said, "To tell the truth, I don't quite know. But I'm all right. I had trouble with the boat and had to put her ashore."

"I'm so sorry," she said. "Shall we be expecting you?"

"Not this time, Susie, I'm afraid. I've got to do some minor repairs, and I think when I've done them, I'd better make for home. I can't expect to do more than a patch-up here. I'll ring you when I yet back, shall I?"

"Oh, please do. You worry the life out of me, going on the way you do."

"No need to worry, Susie. You haven't raised the alarm, have you? I mean told the coastguards or the police or anything?"

"Not yet, no. I wanted to, but Bill said wait till morning. We knew you'd left home, because Bill telephoned, but we couldn't find out if you'd actually sailed."

"That's fine," I said. "Bill was right. Tell him so from me, will you? Well—see you some time, Susie. And I'll ring you when I get back."

"Yes, all right, Pete. Good-bye for now, then."

I said, "'Bye, Susie," and heard her put the receiver down. I kept mine to my ear for a moment or two before I put it down, and heard for the second time that faint click on the line. I put it down then and stood for a moment, thinking, in the total silence. Then I opened the door and went back into the sitting-room.

Mrs. Barlow was sitting on a sofa, half-lit by a shaded standard lamp. We looked at each other for a moment, and then she smiled. "All right?" she said.

"Yes," I said. "No panic. And no one's looking for me."

"That's right. Now, when did you last eat?"

26

"Not for some time, in fact. And then only tea and sandwiches."

She got up. "Well, you can't sleep on that," she said. "I'll get you something. You'd like a drink first. Whisky?"

"Bless you," I said. "Yes, please."

She went over to a side table, where the bottles were, and I stood and watched her. Letty, I thought. Laetitia, presumably. Was anyone ever christened Laetitia these days? She could have been Laetitia Dale, too, give or take a century's change of fashion. There was the same dark beauty a little the worse for wear and, unless I was mistaken, the same toughness underlying the soft manner. I was inclined to like her enormously, but there was a lot you did not know about her, as there was about her husband. She said, "There's only water, I'm afraid. Derek drinks gin, but then he's a sailor."

"Water's what I like," I said, "but then I'm a Scot, sort of."

She turned and brought the glass over to me, and as she did so, I heard the stairs creak again as Barlow came down. I had got one thing right about him, at least. But then it was a thing he did not try to hide. He had all the marks. She said, "Why only sort of, with your name?"

"Well," I said, "I wasn't born here and haven't been here much. I'm only a recent import."

She nodded. "We've been here twelve years," she said. She did not mean it to show, but there was a sudden desolation in the way she said it. Then she said, "Well, you sit down and drink that quietly, and I'll go and see what I can find you to eat."

I took the glass and said again, "Bless you." She looked at me for a moment, and then went out by the door into the hall. The kitchen would be at the other side of the house, or perhaps at the back. I sat down where she had been sitting, because it seemed the nicest place to sit. I sat there in the lamp light, drinking the whisky slowly and looking about me, as you do when you are left alone in a strange room. The whisky was good, and she had given me plenty of it, with an equal quantity of water. Wherever she came from, she knew about that. It was a pleasant room, comfortable but not undistinguished. The furniture was old and good, and there were old sailing prints on the walls. I do not know much about prints, but I thought those looked good, too. There was money here, in a quiet sort of way, probably family money. A couple of minutes later the door from the hall opened and Barlow came in.

He said, "Ah, Letty's given you a drink, good. What about food?"

"I think she's getting me something," I said. "I hope I'm not keeping you up."

"No, no, we don't go to bed early." He had a big, square face, brown with red under it, and wide blue eyes. He had been very fair, but was now grizzled. He said, "I'll join you, I think. Good excuse for a night-cap." He poured himself a drink and came over and sat in an armchair opposite me. His chair, obviously, from the way he fitted into it. He had a very good glassful, but I did not know how much of it was water. You cannot tell with gin. Sailor or no sailor, there was no pink in it. "Still," he said, "you'll be tired after your adventures, so you'll be ready for bed when you've had something to eat. Then in the morning we'll see about your repairs. What are you going to need, do you think?"

We discussed the details for a bit, and he seemed to think he could find me what I wanted. We spoke of nothing else. We asked no questions about each other and told each other nothing. It was all perfectly pleasant and easy. It was only afterwards, when you thought how much had not been said, that it struck you as curious. Then Mrs. Barlow came in and stood in the open doorway. "Ready," she said. "You don't mind the kitchen?"

I said, "Of course not," and got up and followed her. We went into the second door on the other side of the hall. It was a nice kitchen, all white, and warm with a slow-burning stove of some sort. The table was plain wood. I wondered if Barlow holystoned it daily, or whether his wife did it under his supervision. He followed us to the door of the kitchen and then said, "I'll go and see to your room." He shut the door and I heard him go upstairs.

I sat down at that scrubbed table and ate what Mrs. Barlow gave me. I was, in fact, extremely sleepy by now, and the whisky on a near-empty stomach had deepened the pleasurable haze in which I ate. It was something warm out of a casserole, and I thought it tasted marvellous. Here again there was only the one light burning, concentrated on the table top. I sat in the white glare of it, conscious of her pale face watching me from the outer shadow. We said nothing but the bare necessities.

I had just finished eating when Barlow came to conduct me upstairs. Mrs. Barlow and I wished each other good-night as solemnly as we had shaken hands when I arrived. By the time Barlow left me and went downstairs again, I was interested in nothing but bed. But I still wondered. I had lived in a house with a telephone extension in one of the bedrooms. I knew that click on the line. I also knew that a man does not go upstairs to take his waders off. I wondered why Barlow had found it necessary to listen to what I had to say to Susie, and whether he was satisfied with what I had said. But I did not wander about it for long.

Chapter Four

Barlow said, "Well, is that everything you'll want, do you think?"

"Should be," I said.

He got a haversack off a hook on the wall. "Put it all in this," he said. "Then we'd better get moving."

We were in his workshop, which was in an outbuilding at the side of the house. It was better, at least for my purposes, than a farm workshop. It was a mechanical workshop, amateur but efficient, and there was boating gear too. He would have a boat, of course, but I thought it would be power, not sails, or at least a sailing boat with a pretty powerful auxiliary. It is, after all, a long time since the Navy has had to know much about sail, and sailing is very much a matter of taste. That was another of the things I had not asked him. I had not seen a boat anywhere, but with this deeply indented shoreline and all that greenery everywhere, there was no reason why I should. I said, "I'll just go to the house and say good-bye to your wife."

"All right," he said. "You do that." We went out of the workshop and he shut the door behind us. Then I left him standing there and went into the house. I was quite determined to, and in any case the merest courtesy demanded it. I know now that if I had not, the thing would have finished that day. It was because I did not want it to that I was so determined, but of course I could not know then what it would involve.

Mrs. Barlow was in the kitchen, where we had all breakfasted. She looked much better by daylight than she had the night before, and there could be only one explanation of that. She had made herself look better. I do not mean that she was heavily made up or carefully coiffeured, but she had done what was necessary and I could not, willingly, take my eyes off her. I was enormously touched and pleased that she had done that, and I wondered whether Barlow had noticed it. You have to know a couple very well to know how much a husband notices about his wife. Of course it might perfectly well be routine, or she might be going out somewhere. But I did not think so. I said, "I must be going. Thank you very much for everything."

"I've enjoyed it," she said, and that made me think, too, because I knew she meant it, and I wondered about the implications.

I said, "I hope we can meet again."

For what seemed a very long time she looked at me. It was one of the things you noticed about her. So few women look at you for any time at all without saying anything. Then she said, "Well, don't come to the island." It could have been the merest pleasantry, but I thought she meant that, too.

I laughed, to show that it need be no more than a pleasantry if that was all she meant it for. "I won't," I said, "I promise. But I do travel by land as well."

"Yes," she said. She was thinking hard and looking at me all the time. Then she said, "Well, we're in the phone book."

31

"I'm on the phone," I said, "but it's a different name. It's Pennington 366. I live in Pennington." It was the first time the fact had been mentioned.

"All right," she said. "You'd better go now, or you'll miss the ebb. And Derek will be waiting."

"Yes," I said, "all right. Good-bye, and thank you again."

"Good-bye," she said. She had not moved at all. We talked across the scrubbed kitchen table. Then I took my eyes off hers and turned and went out.

Barlow was waiting outside. He was wearing ordinary gumboots, and I was wearing a borrowed pair he said he would take back with him. I had my sailing clothes on and my ropesoles in the top of my kitbag. I slung the kitbag over one shoulder and the haversack over the other, and we set off down the drive. We walked side by side until we got to the beach, but we did not say anything. I had got used to this now. He seemed to be a man who did not say anything unless there was something which, at any particular moment, absolutely needed saying. The silent service perhaps. At any rate, he managed to make it seem perfectly natural.

It was full ebb, with a wide expanse of mud between the island and the mainland. From the beach it dipped slightly towards the centre of the channel and then rose again towards the island. Barlow had talked of a causeway, but I could not see any indication of one. I thought perhaps as the tide came in you would see the link narrow to a line of marginally higher and presumably harder going, with the rock close up under it, but there was nothing of the sort to be seen now, just a flat expanse with that curious satiny sheen on it which is so different from the look of sand. The sky was dappled grey and the wind light but steady from the south-east. A good home wind for me, if once I got afloat, but the effect now was a little cheerless. It ruffled the leaves of the trees and shrubs that grew densely over the whole slope of land above the beach and right up to the ringwall round the house. When we came out on to the beach, the sea seemed far away, and the shore was quieter than the land.

We walked some way eastwards along the beach before we turned off to cross the mud. I remembered that the night before we had seemed to be walking on shingle for quite a time before we came to the road, but it had not occurred to me then that we were walking along the beach and not up it. I had been following that mesmeric spot of light too long through the misty gloom, and my sense of direction had given up the struggle. When Barlow did take to the mud, I could see nothing to show what had made him do it at that particular point. There were no marks anywhere, so that I even wondered for a moment whether they could have been deliberately removed. Surely when the house on the island had been inhabited, the causeway would have been marked. From where we were I could see the beach on the near side of the island, with the track running up from it, and I knew that that was where we must finish up. But I did not expect our line across the mud to be a straight one, and it was not. It followed a long irregular curve. Barlow walked steadily in front of me, with his eyes always ahead. I thought he was probably working on a series of bearings, say from a point on the island to various points on the land where it curved round the island east of it, but I could not see anything that looked like marks deliberately set up. Perhaps after twelve years he simply knew it by instinct. So far as I was concerned, I knew I could never fix the line in my mind with any hope of remembering it. In any case, there was no reason why I should. Letty Barlow had told me not to come to the island, and there was nothing about it I liked. All I wanted was to get my boat off it and not come back. The house on shore, and the woman who lived in it, were a different matter.

As I already knew, the house on shore and the house on the island were in full view of each other, though they stood half back to back, but by the time we were near the landing beach the house on the island had disappeared round the green hump. I thought that when we got up on top of the island, it must be visible, though not very near, and not fully on any skyline. I had seen no sign of it on our walk across the island during the night, but then I had not been looking for it. I thought it was the house, really, that I did not want to see again if I could help it. The island would have been all right without it, but the house tainted the whole place. I wondered if I dare break into Barlow's silence to ask him about it. It would be better if I could talk to somebody about it, even to the uncommunicative Barlow. I could have asked Letty Barlow about it, but I had not had the chance.

When we got on to the beach, Barlow said, "May as well take those boots off and leave them here. I'll pick them up on my way back." I pulled the boots off and put them down at the side of the track just above high-water mark. I took off the socks I had been wearing under them and stowed them in the kitbag in place of the ropesoles, which I put on over bare feet. When I was ready, he led off again. We went up the track, but did not make for the highest point of the island. Instead we took a lower line to the left, which I assumed would lead directly to the beach where the boat was. Even so, the top of the house came up suddenly on our right, just the top of it. I looked at it twice as we walked past it, and then took the plunge.

I said, "Is the house ever occupied? It's a marvellous position for anyone who likes that sort of place. In the summer, anyhow."

He checked slightly in his walk, but did not turn round. Even now that we were off the mud he still went ahead and I followed behind. I asked the question of his moving back, and he answered it over his shoulder.

"No," he said, "no. We tried for summer lets at first, but there were no takers. Anyhow, it would be more trouble than it's worth. And it's got a bad name with the locals. Well, the whole island has, really."

"Bad how?" I said.

"Oh—some old story. The usual sort of thing. Two brothers, it's supposed to have been. They may have built the house, I don't know—anyway, they lived there, and there was a quarrel, and one of them killed the other. Then the killer couldn't wait for the ebb to get off the island, and tried to swim for it, and got drowned. Something like that, anyway. The locals won't go there. They say it's haunted, of course. I can't say I've ever seen anything myself, but then I'm not a Scot. Letty is, but she never goes there, or not for years, anyway."

"What is there supposed to be to see?"

"Oh, one of them walks. The murdered one, presumably. He is supposed to be watching for his brother to come back out of the sea. Whether with the worst of intentions, or because he wants to be reconciled I wouldn't know."

I said nothing for a bit. Then we were going down the slope of the island again, and I knew we must be near the boat. The house was no longer in sight. I said, "You keep it up, anyway."

35

He checked again, and then went on. "The house?" he said. "Well, I just about keep a roof on it. You can't just let a place go. Or I can't, anyway. But I have to do it myself. Now—there's the boat. She looks all right. Let's see." He looked at his watch. "I think I won't wait, if you don't mind. I don't want to have to wait for the night ebb to get back, and you wouldn't want to have to put in and put me ashore."

"Of course," I said. "What about the tools?"

"Oh—hang the bag on one of the bushes over the beach. It won't hurt, and I'll find it tomorrow."

I thought. "There's one thing," I said. "I'm not sure how much tide there'll be, and I might not be able to get her off the beach single-handed."

We were on the beach now. He stood for a moment looking at the boat. "Got an anchor?" he said.

"Yes."

"Plenty of warp?"

"As much as I'm ever likely to need in these waters."

He nodded. "Well, I tell you what," he said. "We'll get her down now as far as the top of the mud. You can still work on her there. Then I'll take the anchor out on to the mud, with all the warp out and any spare line you've got added to it. Then as soon as she's afloat, you can warp her out clear of the rocks. Get sail up first, of course, and then once you've picked up your anchor, you're away. It'll be easier than sailing her out, anyway."

It was the perfect solution. I had not thought of it, and I was really grateful to him. "That'll be fine." I said, "if you don't mind. How long shall I have before the tide's up to her?"

"Oh—a couple of hours, perhaps. That should be enough, if you can do the job at all."

"Plenty," I said. "And I can do it all right—enough to get me home, anyway."

"Right," he said. "Well, let's move her, then."

She was a heavy old boat, and we could have done with rollers, but we got her down at last. Barlow was stronger than I was, and knew more about moving boats. Then I got the anchor out of the bows. I had another seven or eight fathom of spare line strong enough for the job—it did not in fact have to be very strong—and we added that to the top of the warp and made it fast through the fairlead at the bows.

"Right," he said. "Now I'll take the anchor out. I've got the boots and I know the mud." He put the anchor over his shoulder, with the warp trailing behind him, and set out seawards between the two walls of rock.

"Don't get stuck," I said.

"I won't," he said. "When I find I can't get any further, I'll bed the anchor in and come back. But I should be able to get it far enough."

I watched him go. After a little the going got heavier, and he walked with a sort of forward crouch, taking short steps and never letting one foot rest longer than he could help. It looked rather like skiing. When the warp was all out, and about a third of the spare line, I saw him pause for a moment. He was clear of all but the last rocks now. Then he threw the anchor point first into the mud and turned almost without stopping and was on his way back. It was a very competent, assured performance altogether. When he was back on the beach, I said, "I'm enormously grateful to you. I'm not sure I could have managed that, even if I'd thought of it." I was almost desperately anxious not to pretend with this professional.

"No," he said. "Well, you've got to know the mud." He

looked at his watch again. "I'll be off," he said. "Good luck to you, and a fair voyage home."

"Thank you," I said. I did not say anything to him about meeting again. He did not invite it, and it was not him I wanted to see anyway.

He waved good-bye and was off up the track. I looked after him for a moment and then got down to work. I worked steadily, concentrating on the job in hand. I was not in any serious sense working against time, but there was an absolute deadline to be met. I did not think about the island at all. It hung over me, but did not interfere with my work. It was absolutely quiet on the beach now that the human voices had stopped talking. You could feel the wind, but it made no sound in the thorn-bushes. I did not even hear any gulls crying, though you would have thought that this was just the place for them. When I talked to myself, as I tend to do over any sort of a practical job, I talked almost in a whisper. I did not think anyone was watching me. I had not come in off the sea this time, and I was no longer of any interest to anyone, alive or dead.

The job went very much as I had expected. What it came to was that I managed fairly easily a repair which was far from perfect, but which was good enough to get me home, where it could be done again, and this time properly. I had no decisions to make, because I had known in advance what I could do and what I could not do where I was. My only worry was in case some small accident, something like a broken drill or a split wood block, made it impossible for me to do the job at all. Even that would not have been a physical disaster. I could have got the boat up the beach again as the tide rose, and buoyed the anchor warp somehow if I had to leave it behind. But it would have meant either signalling for help on the night ebb or spending the night on the island and awaiting Barlow's return to collect his tools next morning, and the thought of either appalled me. As it was, I had no need to worry. I did the job slowly and carefully, and by the time it was finished, the tide was coming to me steadily across the mud and the anchor already well covered.

Then I got sail up. It was an odd business doing it on a beached boat, but there was no difficulty in it. She sat there with the sails flapping gently in the breeze. The rudder was unshipped and lying in the stern-sheets, but I knew I could ship it again on its new fixings when I had water under me. Then I simply sat on the beach and waited for the tide. I should have had time for a quick exploration of the island, but I did not want to explore it now. All I wanted was to get away from it. I should have liked to have a last look at the house on shore but that would have meant going up on to the island.

When the water was up to the bows, I got into the boat dry-shod, took a strain on the anchor line and sat waiting for her to lift. There was a slight swell coming on to the beach, but there was no reason why she should bump at all, because if I had enough strain on the line, she would edge forward the moment she lifted and there would soon be nothing under her but mud. In fact it all happened much sooner and more easily than I had expected. After a bit I stood in the bows straining steadily on the line, and I took it in the first few times she moved. The next time I found she was free. There could be no more than a few inches of water under the stern, but she was afloat. I pulled the warp in steadily, and we moved out slowly between the black walls of rock.

When we were nearly clear, I made the warp fast, took in the starboard sheet of the foresail and jammed it in the

cleat and shipped the rudder. Then I pulled in the rest of
the warp, and the moment I felt the anchor lift, I rushed
it on board, dumped it anyhow in the bows and nipped
back to the tiller and mainsheet. A moment later we were
sailing. I headed out south-west, almost across the wind.
When I was far enough out, I reckoned I could turn and
run almost all the way home. But for the moment what I
wanted was to get out to sea.

It was some time before I turned round to look astern,
and by then the island had melted back into the land
again, so that it did not look like an island at all. Then I
had nothing to do but sail the boat and think, and it was
not the island I thought about. It was Letty Barlow.

Chapter Five

I thought about her off and on for the whole of the following week. I do not mean that I mooned about like a love-sick youth. I was no longer a youth, and I was not yet anything like lovesick. Also, I had my work to do, which was selling farm machinery. I had taken over the area only a couple of months earlier, and I was finding it hard going. The firm had no doubt sent me because I was Scottish by blood and had a Scots name, but I spoke with an English accent and even my name was Highland, and the Highlands are a long way from here. The man I had taken over from had been a local and knew all the farmers by their Christian names. I sometimes felt I should find it easier selling machinery as an Englishman in France than I did as an Englander in these parts. So my days were fully occupied, and in the evenings I got hold of the bits I wanted and made a proper job of the boat. But in between I thought about Letty Barlow.

The trouble was that I had convinced myself that she was in trouble, or at least unhappy. At best I was sure that she desperately needed company. Living in a place like that with a man like Barlow, I did not see how she could do anything else. And I was strongly enough attracted to her, mentally and physically, to feel that, if she

41

was to have company, it ought to be mine. I was aware of the dangers of this, even as a matter of straight personal relations. I knew that if a woman like that let go, the resulting explosion would be considerable. Human nature being what it is, this made the attraction all the stronger.

Apart from all this, I badly wanted to know more about her—about her and about Barlow and about the whole place. There was a lot there that needed explaining. There was the strong suggestion that Barlow, for all his self-confidence and pleasant manner, was somehow on the defensive, or at least averse to outside company. I did not think this was related directly to his wife. I thought she was the victim of it, merely because she was his wife, but I did not think it was her he was being defensive about. But I could see that any attempt to establish relations with her, even innocent relations, would be seen by him as a threat to his privacy, and would be resented as such. If the relations were less than innocent, his reaction would be doubly powerful, and he was a powerful man. Here too the dangers were apparent. I should not say that I am a person addicted to danger, but most people, one way or another, find any sort of a challenge stimulating, even if it is only a childhood game of chicken.

But I was far from clear how to set about seeing her again. If Barlow had been a farmer, the thing would have been easy, but he was clearly not. When I had put it to her, she had suggested the telephone, but I had the idea that this was not so much an invitation as a warning not simply to chance a visit. I had looked them up in the phone book, of course. The name of the house was Camlet, and the address was simply Carnholm, though they looked a good four miles from it on the map. I had looked them up on the one-inch survey sheet too. The house was not named on the map, as most of the farms were. There was simply the black dot showing the house. Even the island was not given a name of its own, though I thought it must have one locally. I could get there easily enough by road. I could even get to them by sea so long as I had the boat afloat, though I must be taking her in soon for the winter. But I did not think I could get to them at all uninvited, and I did not think the invitation would be forthcoming, even if I asked for it. The decision would be his, not hers, but that was what the decision would be.

I had the boat out the next week-end, but there was no question of sailing to Camlet. My moorings were strictly tidal—there cannot be many on this coast that are not—and I could not easily make that sort of a passage, and pay a visit, and be back on my moorings in one tide. Also, it was starting to blow, and the forecasts were bad. I thought that if this went on, I should have to get the boat in for the season the next week-end. Any spare thought I had during the following week I gave to the boat, which was having a rough time on her moorings. Then at the end of the week the weather quietened, and I decided to give her another week. As soon as the boat was off my mind, I found myself thinking about Letty Barlow again, and on the Tuesday the thing settled itself. I am not saying circumstances forced my hand, but they gave me an opportunity I could not let go. I had to go and see a farmer called McAdam, and the farm was called Clauchrie. When I looked it up on the map, I saw that it was only a couple of miles from Camlet. So when I had finished with the farmer, I could ring up and say I was on business in these parts and might I look in on them? Even if I got Barlow, and even if he put me off, I did not see how he could take it amiss. But of course I hoped it would be Letty Barlow who answered the phone.

Once the wind had dropped, the weather settled into

one of those still, golden stretches which you can get in September on any of the Atlantic coasts, and which are so magical that they make the summer gone and the winter ahead seem equally remote and unimportant. The sun shone every day in a hazy but cloudless sky, the wind never stopped blowing very gently from almost due south, the days were warm but never hot and the nights were moonlit with enormous dews. Whether it was this or the possibility of seeing Letty Barlow again, I suddenly regained my touch with the selling. I think what in fact happened was that I gave up any pretence of being Scots and assumed the pose of an honest Englishman, which the farmers found so novel a conception that they could not help listening to me. Once the customer really listens, the thing is more than half done. That is, so long as the product is sound and the customer reasonably solvent, and our products were first-rate and the local farmers spending money as if it was going out of fashion, which in a sense it was. I had sold Mr. McAdam a complete new milking system before I asked if I might use his telephone for a strictly local call.

I was glad it was a private phone I was using. There is something inhuman and slightly sordid about a call-box, and the way the things work now, this comes through to the receiver as much as to the caller. As it was, I spoke from the slightly stuffy but solid quiet of the farmer's office-room, with only a blue-bottle buzzing in the tight-shut window for company, and when I dialled the number, I heard the bell ring at the other end and then, after a moment or two, Letty Barlow's voice on the line. It was as good on the telephone as it was face-to-face, and that is a great test of a voice. I said, "Mrs. Barlow? It's Peter Grant speaking. Your late ship-wrecked mariner."

She said, "Oh." Then there was quite a pause. I

thought if I had been there, she would have been looking at me in the way she did. I also wondered if she was wondering where Barlow was. I thought she would know if he was upstairs and could see him if he was down. All the same, I kept my ear strained for that click on the line. I suppose all this thinking took about three seconds flat. Then she said, "Good-afternoon, Mr. Grant. How are you? And where are you?"

"I'm well," I said, "thank you. So's the boat. And I'm at Clauchrie, only a couple of miles from you. I'm here on business, and as it's so close, I wondered if I might come over." Even with her I kept to the proper patter. I had heard no click, but I still could not be sure that I had her to myself.

She said, "Oh" again. I thought it sounded a little breathless, but that may have been my over-heated imagination. Then she said, "I'm not sure—" She did not say what she was not sure of, but I knew without her telling me, and I did not wait for her to go on.

I said, "Don't bother if it's difficult. Only I'd like to see you." I blessed, as I have so often blessed before, the English "you," which is both singular and plural.

"Well, as a matter of fact," she said, "I've got to go into Carnholm to shop."

I thought that just possibly she had been doing some quick thinking too. I said, "Well, that's almost on my way home. Perhaps we could meet there?"

"All right," she said. "That would be nice. I shan't have long, I'm afraid."

I said, "Never mind. Where?"

"I always park by the clock-tower," she said. Every small town has its clock-tower here. I do not know why, but it is one of the first things you notice. "It's a green Renault Six. If I'm not in the car, I shan't be away long."

"When, then?"

"In about half an hour? No, say three-quarters. I don't want to keep you waiting."

"Three-quarters of an hour from now at the clock-tower," I said. "Till then."

She said, "All right," and put the receiver down.

It was difficult to say why, but the whole thing had the feeling of a clandestine conversation, and I did not think clandestine conversations were very much in Letty Barlow's line. I found my heart beating with ridiculous emphasis. Then I put the receiver down and went out to make my farewells with Mr. McAdam. I had still heard no click on the line.

I did not need three-quarters of an hour to get to Carnholm, but I set off straight away all the same. I had of course fixed no other meetings for the afternoon, and in any case, so far as the job was concerned, I felt I could rest on my battle-honours with Mr. McAdam. So I drove off, with my eyes on the road and my heart in my mouth, to meet Letty Barlow at the Carnholm clock-tower, about six miles away, in three-quarters of an hour's time, and made it, even through the narrow winding roads, with more than half an hour to spare. There was not, of course, any green Renault Six anywhere near the clock-tower, though the car park was full of foreign cars with local number plates. I am not sure if the French and German car-makers have deliberately exploited the Scot's more or less conscious antipathy to the English, but I find it difficult to believe that the ordinary run of people in these parts do not buy foreign much more readily than their counterparts further south. I wondered if my British car and English number plate did not militate against sales almost as much as my English accent, and whether I could persuade head office to let me buy a big new foreigner from a local dealer on the strength of it. I thought perhaps I had better sell a bit more machinery before I suggested it. For the moment I parked my conspicuously English car where I could see a green Renault Six the moment it entered the car park. Then I sat and waited for it. It arrived, with a local number plate and Letty Barlow at the wheel, exactly seventeen minutes later. I know, because I timed it. I let it settle, and then got out and walked over to it.

She was collecting things from the seat beside her, as you do before getting out of the car to do almost anything, but when she saw me coming, she left them and sat there in the driving seat looking at me, as if she had not quite made up her mind to get out of the car at all. I stood beside the car and looked down at her, and she looked up at me, through the car window. I said, "Hullo." I could not bring myself, now that I knew I had her to myself, to call her Mrs. Barlow, but I did not want to chance my arm with Letty. She was not a person you assumed anything with, anything at all.

She said, "Hullo, Peter. May I call you Peter?"

"Please. May I call you Letty? I really rather fancy calling you Laetitia, but I don't even know if that's your name."

"It is, in fact," she said, "but I doubt if anyone's ever called me by it, at any rate since the christening. I'm not at all sure it suits me, anyway."

"It suits you very well," I said.

She looked at me suspiciously. "You don't mean Laetitia Dale, do you?" she said.

I surrendered. "I did rather. Are you a Meredith fan, too?"

"Mere*d*ith," she said, giving the word its proper Celtic stress on the second syllable. "Not really, but of course

I've been dogged by it all my life. Only I'm not sure I like the association."

"Never mind. I can't pretend I read any of the others much, I must say. But that one's very good reading, say what you like. All right, let's keep it at Letty for the moment. We can discuss the associations of Laetitia later."

She said, "I really have got shopping to do, you know. Not much, but I must do it."

She said it very pointedly, and I said, "Good God, I know you have. And I'm very early. May I shop with you, or shall I wait while you do it?"

She looked at me with a small touch of real distress. "I think better not, if you don't mind," she said. "I shan't be long."

I said, "Of course." I could not bear to see her looking at me like that. "I'll wait in my car and look out for you." I turned and walked back to my car, and by the time I got to it, she was out of hers and had disappeared into the one long shopping street Carnholm possesses.

She was gone longer than I expected. I wondered how long it was since I had sat in my car like this, waiting for someone to find time for me. I certainly would not do it for the customers. When she did appear, she was carrying a good deal of stuff. There was nothing improvised about her shopping trip, but then I had not really thought there was. She was stowing it in the back of the car when I came over to her. She shut the rear door down and turned and looked at me. "Where, then?" I said.

"Come and sit in the car," she said. "It's quiet, but comfortably public." She got into the driving seat and I got in on the other side. Then she turned and looked at me again.

She said, "I know your name, and that you live at Pennington, but haven't been there long."

"Two months," I said.

"What do you do there?"

I told her. She nodded. "And that's what brought you out to Clauchrie this afternoon?"

"That's right," I said. "I left Mr. McAdam a poorer but wiser man, but much better equipped, or soon will be. I mean, I didn't engineer the visit to these parts. It happened in the course of trade, and I just took advantage of it."

"I see." She thought for a moment. Then she said, "You're not married or anything?"

"Not even anything," I said.

"And you live by yourself?"

"At the moment I've taken over my predecessor's house. But he was a married man, and it's much too big for me. I'll find something smaller if I can. And quieter. I'm not all that keen on Pennington. I'd like to be more on my own and a bit nearer the sea." She nodded, but did not say anything. I said, "And you've lived at Camlet for twelve years?"

"That's right," she said. "Quiet and by the sea."

I answered the tone rather than the words. "You don't like it?" I said.

She was not looking at me now. She sat staring out through the windscreen, though there was nothing to see but parked cars and moving people. "Not now," she said. "It was all right at first."

"What changed it?"

"It wasn't it that changed, it was us." She turned to me suddenly, almost fiercely. "Look," she said, "I'm not just the ordinary bored wife looking for a flutter. You do understand that? If that's what you're thinking, I'd rather not see you again."

I looked at her very straight. "I think you're a bored

49

wife," I said, "bored, if nothing worse. But I don't think you're ordinary, and I don't think you're looking for a flutter, and I wasn't proposing to flutter with you. I think you're lonely, and I suspect you're unhappy, and I like you very much. I liked you the moment I saw you, and more still when I heard you speak. If there's anything I can do, tell me. If nothing, I won't bother you again."

"You don't bother me," she said. "I needn't have met you this afternoon if I hadn't wanted to, need I?"

"All right. Let's say, with all proper qualifications, that you are prepared to like me. Now, that being so, what, if anything, can I do for you?"

She said, "Just talk to me sometimes."

"But not at Camlet?"

She looked away from me again. She said, "Derek doesn't like visitors."

"He was very kind to me," I said. "I mean, really kind. I couldn't have done without him. Only it didn't feel like kindness. At least, I couldn't tell what he was feeling."

"You can't," she said. "But he wanted you off the place."

"Off the island?" I said.

She said, "Well, it was the island you were on," and for the first time I felt she was fencing with me.

"All right," I said. "To hell with the island, if it isn't there already. I haven't the least wish to go to it again, and it wasn't my choice in the first place."

She looked at me again with that distress in her face, and again I did not know how to bear it. "I know that," she said. "I'm sorry."

"Letty, Letty," I said, "there's nothing to be sorry for. Look, if we're to meet, I must be able to get in touch with you somehow. Or shall I leave it to you? You can telephone me, only I'm out most of the day. Or you could write. Could I write to you?"

"Oh, I think so," she said. "I get quite a lot of letters. I'm one of the few people left who still write them. And Derek's not that sort of a husband, if that's what you're thinking." She looked at her watch. "I must be going," she said. "Leave it to me, will you? You're Pennington 366, only it's under another name."

I got out of the car. "That's right," I said. "All right, Letty. I leave it to you, very happily."

She said, "Bless you, Peter," and I shut the door of the car.

I watched her drive out of the car park, and then walked back to my own car. I did not know what to make of it all, but I knew that my peace of mind had gone, and that I was at Letty Barlow's mercy. But I did not mind either.

Chapter Six

I was at Clauchrie again a couple of days later. There were details to be settled with Mr. McAdam, but this time I did not telephone Camlet. When we had finished what we had to do, I said, "What's that island called, just off the coast?" I jerked my head vaguely southeastward.

Mr. McAdam looked at me. "Island?" he said.

"That's right. There's an island just off the coast a couple of miles from here. It's not very big. What's it called, do you know?"

"Oh, ay," he said, "there's a wee island right enough. I think maybe they had a name for it, but I canna call it to mind. I havena heard it spoken of in years."

"Who owns it, then? Somebody must."

He looked puzzled. "I think maybe it would be Mr. Barlow's at Camlet," he said, "but I'm no precisely sure."

"There's a house on it," I said. "Doesn't anyone live there?"

He smiled at me. I thought he had almost laughed at the daftness of my question. "Och," he said, "who'd want to live in a place like that the noo? I mind there was an old man living there one time, that used to have sheep on the island, but that's years back. People won't live in a place like that any more, unless it was one of these visi-

52

tors camping, with tents and that." His little joke came out in the open. He said, "You're no thinking of settling there yourself?"

I laughed heartily with him. The customer is always right. "To tell the truth," I said, "I think it would rather suit me, but I don't think the head office would be best pleased."

"Ah, well," said Mr. McAdam, "maybe not." The joke had run its course, but we were very friendly and pleased with each other.

I said, "No, only I was told there were two brothers had it at one time. There was some story about them." I let my voice trail off expectantly, but his face was a blank.

"Brothers?" he said. "I never heard of any brothers there. When would this be, then?"

I was all vagueness and deprecation. "Oh, I don't know," I said. "Way back, I suppose. Some chap told me."

He shook his head firmly. He said again, "I never heard of any brothers there."

I nodded. "And how long have you been farming Clauchrie, Mr. McAdam?"

He said, "By my own self since my father died, and with him before that. I was born here, and I'm no so young as I was."

I paid him the necessary compliments on his fitness, and took my leave, and drove slowly through the lanes towards Carnholm. I wondered who was fooling whom, and why. Above all, I wondered why. And yet I had been on the island, which Mr. McAdam, so far as appeared, had not. I had seen that house in the grey dusk, and I could have believed anything. When I got to Carnholm, I drove, quite deliberately, to the clock-tower and looked in the car park for a green Renault Six. I did not think that was against the terms of the treaty. But there was no green Renault there, and I headed back towards Pennington.

The weather was still perfect, and when I had had my supper, I telephoned the Marlings at Canty Port. I got Bill this time. He said, "Oh, hullo, Pete. How's the boat?"

I said, "All shipshape and Bristol-fashion."

He said, "Bristol's a long way from here. You'd better watch your step."

"For God's sake," I said, "in this weather? What about this week-end?"

"We'd love to see you, but why not come by road? Then we'd be sure of you."

"You must be joking," I said. "You know what the roads are like at the week-ends in these parts. Every other driver you meet full to the eyebrows. I'm safer at sea."

He sighed. "All right," he said. "It's up to you. You seem to be a lucky sailor, at least."

I thought in a way I was, though I did not tell him why. "Right," I said. "I'll be seeing you."

He said, "I hope so," and we rang off. Bill was no sailor, lucky or unlucky, and he had no faith in boats.

I got away early on the Saturday morning. I was equipped exactly as I had been a fortnight before, with two exceptions. I had my field-glasses and I had the Ordnance Survey sheet covering the coast between Vance and Canty Port. What is much more to the point, I carried a very clear picture of it in my head. I had the sheet with me for verification if necessary, but I reckoned this time I knew in detail what to look for and what to do about it. For inshore sailors like myself, the Ordnance Survey sheet is as good as an Admiralty chart.

That divine weather still held. The breeze was light but rock-steady, so that after a bit I even made the mainsheet fast, and sat comfortably with a casual hand on the tiller, watching the coastline unfold as we moved slowly across it. The inshore hills were putting on their autumn colours now, and in the calm, slightly misty sunlight the whole world was gold and pale green. The small-boat sailor, despite his reputation, is not necessarily a masochist, and when he gets his pleasure unalloyed, it is of a very rarefied kind, especially if he sails singlehanded, with no one to pretend to.

This time I saw the island coming. It still looked like a headland, a small headland with a wooded belt inland of it, which is common enough round here, but I knew now that it was the trees that marked the real coastline. When I was well to the west of it, I turned almost on to the wind and sailed straight in, with the breeze under my starboard quarter, aiming at the gap between the island and the land west of it. I was not so mad as to think of trying to sail inside it. I did not really know how much water there was, and with a wind as light as this, I might find myself in difficulties when I got under its lee. To sail through that passage might be an adventure, but to find myself drifting there did not bear thinking about. But I wanted to get in close enough to see the way in, and if possible to see Camlet itself. I did not expect, even with the glasses, to see Letty Barlow waving to me out of a top window, but at least I wanted to see the house.

It is difficult to judge distances across the sea, or I find it so, and I should not like to be precise about how far out I was when I suddenly opened the passage and saw Camlet standing there, looking across at its island, with the greenery all round it except to seaward, and the beach at its foot, and the water well up on the beach. Once I could see it, I made everything fast as it was and got the glasses out for a better look. I could see it all very clearly, but it

55

was still a long way away. If someone had really been waving out of a top window, or even moving across the back of the house, I should have seen them all right, but anyone could have been standing inside one of the windows without my seeing them at all. I suddenly had an unnerving picture of Derek Barlow standing there with a telescope to his eye, watching me watching his house through my glasses out of my small boat, and I put the glasses down quickly beside me and turned back to my steering. The boat was still sailing steadily towards the land with the wind under her starboard quarter, but now I loosed the sheets and took the tiller and wore her right round through a hundred and eighty degrees, till the wind was on her port bow. Then I sheeted in, changed sides and settled down to sail as near the wind as I could get until I was far enough out to turn across it again and head for Canty Port. I could not say what I had accomplished. For what it was worth, I had established to my satisfaction that, given the tide and the right wind, I could sail straight in and beach the boat under Camlet if I wanted to. Perhaps I could even sail on round the island and come out on its eastern side. But when I might want to do either, and why, I did not know.

It was only when I was heading out to sea again that it occurred to me that I had not seen the house on the island. I thought it must be further down and further round the landward side than I had allowed for, though it could well be that I could have seen the roof or chimneys if I had looked for them. As I sat now, I had my back to the island, but with this thought in mind I turned instinctively to look at it over my shoulder. Whatever I could have seen from further in, I could see nothing of the house now at all. It was just as I was turning round to look seaward again that I saw movement on the seaward

56

face of the island. It happened exactly as it had that first time when I had been holding my boat in the surf on the beach, only then it had been something motionless and relatively near at hand and now it was moving, but a long way away. I took tiller and sheet in one hand and leaned across the boat and grabbed the glasses with the other. Then I turned again with the glasses to my eyes.

Like that, everything was very unsteady. A boat sailing into the wind always moves more than a boat running, even if the sea is calm, and even on land you cannot hold a big pair of glasses very steady with one hand. But I did get a glimpse of a figure as my field of vision swung across the nearer end of the island, and I had no doubt whose figure it was. The tall broad body in dark clothes with the fair head on top of it was unmistakable. He was moving sideways across a slope, low down close to the water, where he would be visible from the sea but not from the land. This time there was nothing to suggest that he was watching me. His face did not seem to be turned in my direction. Then the boat came up into the wind, and I had to put the glasses down quickly at my feet and bring her back on course again. When she was steady, I tried one more quick look, but could see nothing, only the bare green slopes with the black rocks at their foot, and at one point a little eastward the dark opening of the tiny bay where I had beached the boat a fortnight before.

The rest of the voyage was uneventful. There was, as I had thought, no mistaking Canty Port when I opened it, and I had a fair wind into it. Just outside the little harbour mouth I got the mainsail down and fixed the foresail to give me steerage way through the boats moored inside. The harbour is tidal, but it empties only at full ebb, and there was plenty of water left when I came in past the stone pier head. I was far from certain what to do about mooring the boat and getting ashore, and I had left this to be decided when I got there. If there was anyone helpful about with a pram or rowing boat, I thought I might anchor in the middle and ask him to put me ashore, but I could not see anyone likely. There were one or two real yachts, sea-going ships by my standards, and one had a pram alongside, as if the owner was aboard, but I am chary of asking favours of proper yachtsmen. The owner might be sleeping off a long hard day at sea or a long hard night ashore, or even, yachtsmen being what they are, in bed with his crew. Having little time to decide, I settled for going well in, anchoring, waiting for the rest of the ebb and then walking ashore over the mud, and this is what I finally did. By the time I had got the sails down and properly stowed and made all fast aboard, there was only a foot of water under me, and when it had dropped to six inches, I put my shoes in the kitbag, put the kitbag on my shoulder, rolled my trousers up above the knee and swung a leg overboard.

I had reckoned without the Canty Port mud. It was not deep, but it was sticky, full of strange solids and unspeakably foul. It was thus that I arrived at the Marlings' door barefoot, no doubt a picturesque seafaring figure, but stinking like a polecat from the knees down. Susie screamed cheerfully when she saw me, and Bill took one look at me, tutted audibly, and led me firmly to an outside tap. Under his supervision I washed myself, put my ropesoles on over still wet feet, rolled down my trousers over still wet shins and was finally admitted to the house.

We made a very cheerful evening of it. We all had a good deal to drink, and when they asked me about my abortive voyage of the fortnight before, I gave them the full treatment, with Susie, who for all her silliness was an attractive little woman, with large green eyes and a sympathetic manner, playing Desdemona to perfection. She swore 'twas strange, 'twas passing strange, 'twas pitiful, 'twas wondrous pitiful, until with a lot of whisky inside me I began to wonder whether she might not be persuaded to love me for the dangers I had passed, only there was not the slightest opportunity of finding out, and in any case I was too fond of Bill to try it. I named no names in my tale of heroism and adventure, partly because I did not want to mar it with too much fact, but also because I had by now, drunk or sober, become instinctively cagey on the whole subject of Camlet. There was a lot that I understood so little myself that I shrank from trying to explain it to other people, even Bill and Susie. Above all, of course, there was Letty Barlow. I did not want to discuss her with anyone. But when Bill asked me point-blank, I did not see how I could dodge it. Even on my embroidered version of the facts, I could not expect him to believe that I had parted company with my rescuers without learning their names. And Bill, though not a native, had been living in these parts a long time.

He re-filled my glass and said, "You're a good liar, Pete, I must say, but I suppose some of it happened. Who were these people, do you know?"

I lashed around a bit in my whiskified mind, but I told myself I could trust Bill if anyone. "Oh," I said, "people called Barlow. At least, I think that's right. We didn't go in for the formalities much."

Bill nodded, and I saw his eyes go to Susie's for a moment and then come back to mine. "Barlow?" he said. "Big chap, naval type of some sort, with a pretty wife?"

I put on a fair show of judicious consideration. "Big certainly," I said. "Naval could be. He seemed to know about boats all right, but so do all sorts of people nowadays. Pretty? Well, all right, but not a glamour puss exactly. Very quiet, both of them."

Bill said, "Oh come off it, Pete. You'd think any woman pretty if she didn't actually squint and had all the usual things in roughly the usual places."

I was full of mock indignation, but at the back of my mind, even in its present confused state, I knew that I wanted to hear what Bill could tell me. I said, "Oh, nonsense. I'm very choosey, aren't I, Susie?" Then the rhyme struck me as funny, and I giggled a little.

Susie was a bit away too. She opened her big green eyes and said, "I don't know, Pete. How should I know how choosey you are?"

Bill snorted. I wondered, not for the first time, how much he had to put up with from Susie and her little ways, and how he dealt with it. It is not a thing you discuss with a man, and the better you know him, the less likely you are to discuss it. He said, "Well, Susie remembers the Barlows, don't you, Susie? That is, if they're the same people, and they sound like it. They used to live somewhere between here and Pennington, and maybe they still do."

I was struck by the past tense and this talk of remembering, as if the Barlows were somehow part of their past experience but not of their present. But there was nothing more for me to say. I just sat there and looked at them. Then Bill said, "We used to meet them at one time. They were never special friends of ours, but you met them about the place. And then they sort of faded out, and you didn't seem to see them any more. I didn't give it a lot of thought, but I assumed they'd moved or something."

Susie nodded. "That's right," she said. "I haven't seen them for—I don't know, four or five years, I should think."

"Well, anyway," I said, "there they are, if they are the same people. But maybe they're not."

Susie said, "And she was pretty, Pete. Well, not pretty, perhaps, but very striking. One noticed her. If you really didn't, either you're slipping or else it's not the same woman."

I blinked at her owlishly. I was concerned now to seem a little more drunk than I really was. "Maybe I'm slipping," I said. "It must be my age."

We left it there, and the evening went back to exactly the evening it would have been if I had never gone ashore on that damned island or waited for a green Renault Six by the Carnholm clock-tower. My mind, as a fairly drunken mind will, sealed itself into a small immediate reality, and saw the rest of my experience, when I turned to look at it, quite clearly but insulated from all feeling. I knew about Letty Barlow and my feelings for her as facts, but I was taken up with the companionship of Bill and the immediate attractions of Susie. When at last we agreed that the evening was over, Bill went out into the kitchen to see to the stove or something, and Susie went upstairs to see to things there. I stood in the sitting-room, leaning with one hand on the mantelpiece and trying, left to myself, to get my thoughts into some sort of coherent order again. Then Susie came downstairs and said, "I'm going to bed. Good-night, Pete."

She put up her face to be kissed, as I had kissed it dozens of times before, and then suddenly my arms were round her and we were kissing differently. After a moment she opened her eyes and said, "Oh, Pete," and I let her go and she went upstairs. I still stood there, and a wave of pure physical longing hit me suddenly, so that I almost cried out. But it was not Susie I longed for, it was Letty Barlow, and I had not the slightest doubt that Susie

61

knew that. I wiped my mouth mechanically in case Susie had left too much of her lipstick there, and then Bill came in from the kitchen, and we shut the house up and went upstairs, talking in the curious clipped way men do when they still have drink aboard, but the excitement has died out of it.

I went to bed slowly, thinking in uneven spasms about the day's events. Letty had said they had been all right at first, but then changed, and now here was Bill saying that the Barlows were around everywhere at first and had then seemed to disappear. Four or five years ago, Susie had said. The two bits of the jigsaw fitted together, but I could not see what they represented. Then I thought of Barlow walking on the slope of the island above the water, and something niggled at my mind, but I could not think what was wrong. It was only after I had got into bed that I suddenly knew what it was. It was the tide, of course. When I had passed the island, it must have been near the full flood. The causeway would have been covered for several hours and would not be uncovered for several hours more. Barlow would never have let himself be caught by the tide. Either he had come over by boat, when the causeway was already covered, or he had deliberately arranged to be on the island from one ebb to the next. Admittedly I was not at my clearest-headed, but I could not think of a single reason why he should do either. I did not try very long. I went to sleep almost at once and woke only to a smell of coffee from downstairs.

Chapter Seven

Letty Barlow phoned in the evening the day after I got back. I got quite a lot of phone calls in the evening, because people knew it was about the only time they could be sure of finding me, and they assumed that, not being a family man, I should not mind. But I thought this was Letty as soon as the bell went. All the same, I picked up the receiver and gave my number, just as I always did. There was that short silence, and I knew then for certain that it was Letty. Then she said, "Peter?"

I said, "Yes, Letty. How are you?" I wanted to be friendly and undramatic, but also I wanted to know.

She said, "I'm all right," but she did not sound it.

"You're at home?" I said.

"Oh, yes." I did not ask where Barlow was. I assumed he was out of earshot and nowhere near the upstairs extension, but I could not make the assumption openly, because there was still the convention, not quite the pretence, but the unstated convention, between us that everything was fair and above-board. I did not really think that Letty would have told him of our meeting in Carnholm, though it was just possible that she might have mentioned it as a chance encounter, but I thought she was still telling herself that there was nothing of the intrigue in our relation. Sooner or later, unless I was mistaken, she would have to face the fact that there was more than a touch of it, but I was anxious not to force her hand. She was not built for intrigue, and if circumstances, even her own desperation, forced her into it, she would have to get used to the idea gradually, or a sudden revulsion might drive her away from me altogether. And I wanted her badly now, in any way and on any terms I could get.

There had been a silence, but not a long one, and I was used to her silences. Then she said, "Look, I know you're busy, but I wondered whether you'd be free tomorrow evening—well, early evening, really—after tea, say."

I looked down at the diary I kept beside the phone. Also, because anyone with a boat on a tidal mooring is very conscious of these things, I thought that that would be the time of the ebb, and I wondered if there was any connection. It would not be full ebb till later, but by about five or half-past the tide would be well down. I said, "Yes, I'm free from tea-time onwards."

"Could we meet, do you think?"

"I'd like that very much. Say where and when."

She said, "The trouble is, I mustn't be too far from here, and that means a certain amount of driving for you."

"Never mind that," I said.

"Well—there's a place called Maulness Point a bit east of here. It's marked on the map. I can walk there along the cliff. You can get the car to within a quarter of a mile of it and walk the rest. It's all pretty open. We couldn't miss each other, and I'll be looking out for you. Would you mind awfully?"

I said, "You know very well I shouldn't mind. Letty, you really are all right?"

"Oh yes, I think so. But I'd like to talk to you. Could you be there about half past five?"

"Bar accidents," I said, "I'll be there."

She said, "Bless you, Peter. Till tomorrow, then."

I said, "Till tomorrow," and she rang off.

To do myself justice, I was at least as much worried as I was elated when I put the receiver down. I did not think, now, that this was just a lonely woman, or even an unhappy one, desperate for company. I thought it was a woman in trouble, wanting, if not help, at least someone to talk over her trouble with. I did not, even, let myself think that she had picked on me for my bright eyes or perhaps too obvious admiration. I thought probably I had come into her life, almost literally out of the blue, at just the moment when the pressures on her, whatever they were, were becoming intolerable, or perhaps simply when the merest prudence told her that she must do something. I thought she was a prudent person. I would have betted all I was worth that the emotions ran deep in her, but I was equally certain that she had them well under control. She was the sort of natural antithesis of poor Susie, both in herself and in her situation. She demanded to be taken seriously, and I took her very seriously indeed. I even wondered whether it might not be only herself she was worried about. She could be worried about Barlow, too. For all his strength and competence and silence, Barlow could be a man in trouble. I should not have thought that listening to other people's telephone conversations came naturally to him, any more than matrimonial intrigue did to his wife. I wanted to see Letty desperately, but I was pretty considerably worried over the whole situation.

I believe even if I had gone to Maulness Point by myself that evening, I should still remember it. It was one of the most wonderful evenings I have ever seen. The sun,

65

already low, struck sideways all along that broken coastline, picking out the high spots in misted gold, so that
they seemed to float on the intervening shadow. The wind
had died out completely, and the sea, untouched by either sun or wind, lay in a flat silver sheet under the
dappled land. Away to the south-east, almost lost in the
haze, the English hills repeated very faintly the opales-
cent splendour of the Scottish coast. There was nothing
on the headland but bare turf, sloping steeply to the cliff,
and the air smelt of sea-turf and the sea itself. When I
came out over the top, I saw Letty Barlow at once, a single dark figure at the bottom of the slope, silhouetted
against the sea. She looked utterly forlorn, but I think
anyone would have looked forlorn in that setting.

I walked down towards her, and after a bit she turned
and saw me coming, and started up the slope to meet me.
I was so moved by the sight of her that I dropped my
defences and said what was uppermost in my mind. I
said, "Where's Derek?"

I had not meant the question to worry her, but of
course it did. All the same, I could not be altogether
sorry, because I knew that it was really Barlow we had to
talk about, and I thought the sooner we talked about him,
the better. She said, "Oh—he's out."

"Out on the island?" I said.

She looked at me almost as if I had hit her, but I was
past caring now. My own defences were down, and I
wanted hers down too. She said, "Oh, Peter. Yes, all right,
he's on the island. But how—?"

"It's the ebb," I said. "When else would he go there?"
But even as I said it, I thought that this was not true, because of what I had seen from the boat two days ago. I
said, "Does he go there most days?"

We stood there on the green slope staring at each

other. You could not see the island from here, because a fold of the cliff hid it. Equally, of course, anyone on the island could not see us. I supposed that was why we were where we were. She was looking at me with her eyes very wide open, almost as if she was hypnotised. Her face was quite blank. Then she said, "Most days, yes."

"And that's what you're worried about?"

She gave a very slight nod. "In a way, yes," she said.

I thought for a moment. Then I said, "And he's the only person who can go there? I mean, walk there at the ebb?"

This puzzled her. "Not really," she said. "Why?"

I was puzzled too now. I said, "But isn't he the only person who knows the way across?"

She shook her head. She was still puzzled. "Oh no, not really. Only no one else would want to go there."

Another piece of the jigsaw was beginning to take shape in my mind, but I had to be sure. I said, "But you've got to know the line, haven't you? You've got to know where the causeway is. He—" I checked myself and said, "I thought you couldn't get across unless you knew the exact line?"

"Well, yes, but there's nothing particularly difficult about it." We were off dangerous ground for the moment, and she sounded more reasonable and ordinary. "You just leave the beach at a particular point and walk straight across to the nearest point of the island. They used to drive sheep across in the old days. They must have had good dogs, of course, and I suppose if the tide caught them, they could have lost one or two. But for a man by himself it's safe enough. It's the water that's unsafe. I mean when the tide's in. You couldn't swim it, or not easily. There's a bad tide-race through the passage, except just at slack water, and that doesn't last long."

"I see," I said. I did see, too. I remembered our torchlit walk back to the mainland in the night, and our elaborate manoeuvres by daylight next morning. I thought Barlow had had to get me off the island and then, because my boat was there, had had to get me back on to it, but he had made it all seem as difficult as possible. And you could take a flock of sheep across, that's if you had the dogs. I remembered now Mr. McAdam's saying that an old man used to keep sheep on the island, but it had never occurred to me to wonder how they got there. I also remembered my determination, that first evening, to swim across if no one answered my signals. Barlow had answered my signals, but he had left it pretty late. Only of course he had had to wait for the ebb.

Letty said, "Peter, you won't go there, will you?" That brought us back to the central point again, only now her attitude had changed. I suppose it was my fault, forcing the pace the way I had with direct questions and showing, inevitably, by those very questions that I had already begun edging my way in through the outer defences of the truth. She was having second thoughts now. I think perhaps she had been wanting to talk to me in general terms about her relation with her husband and the effect his secret, whatever it was, was having on her life with him. Now, instead of listening sympathetically as I should have done, I had gone direct for the secret itself, and this she was not prepared for, or not yet.

I said, "Not if I can help it, believe me. I've already told you that. The place frightens the life out of me. I don't know why, but it does."

"Well, stay away from it, then," she said. "I do."

"Because whatever there is there, it's Derek's thing?"

"Yes, if you like. But you mustn't take that the wrong way. Derek keeps me out of it because, whatever it is, it's something he doesn't want me involved in for my sake. You must understand that. He's carrying it himself because he feels he must. I accepted that at the start, only things have changed. For one thing, I don't think he realised—I'm not sure he realises, even now—how destructive a thing like that is to any relation, particularly between husband and wife. Its effect is terrible, on me, anyhow. I don't know about him. I told you, it's so difficult to know what he feels about anything. But the other thing is, I'm afraid it's getting out of hand. I feel it's starting to do him a lot of harm, in himself, I mean, quite apart from his relations with me. And I don't know what I can do about it."

I thought for a moment. "You said 'whatever it is,'" I said. "Do you mean you don't know?"

She looked at me very straight. We were still standing there facing each other, where we had first met. The sunlight was lifting, height by height, from the whole coastline east of us, and we still had not moved. She said, "I know something, of course, because it was inevitable that I should get to know. I don't know anything like the whole of it. And even what I know is never acknowledged between us. It just isn't referred to, though Derek must know I know it. But you see, he trusts me absolutely. And now I'm betraying his trust, talking to you, even to this extent. But I tell you one thing. If he ever had any idea that I had talked to you, or even that you were interested —I don't know what he'd do, but his reaction would be very violent indeed. To this extent at any rate I'm putting myself in your hands, Peter."

I said, "Why my hands, Letty?"

She put out a hand suddenly and touched mine. Her hand was very cold, but still very strong and fine. It was only the second time I had touched her. "Let's face it," she said, "partly because you dropped right into the middle of it, and at the psychological moment when I knew I couldn't go on as I was any longer. But also because I like you very much and trust you. Is that an adequate answer?"

"It satisfies me," I said. "I'm your man, Letty. You know that, don't you? You must know. Whatever happens, I'm your man. And I've never been anyone's before."

She looked at me for what seemed a very long time. Then she gave my hand a little squeeze and took her hand away. "You've picked a pretty rum customer," she said. "Now I must be going. You won't be too late back?"

"Of course not," I said. "And the agreement still holds? I wait on you?"

"Please," she said. "It's the only way."

"All right for the moment," I said. "But don't leave it too late. That's if things are moving as you say. Or I may take the law into my own hands."

"You mustn't," she said. "Believe me, you mustn't. Now I'm going. Good-bye, Peter."

I said, "Good-bye, Letty," and she turned and went off along the cliff. I watched her go a little, and then turned myself and started to walk up the slope to where I had left the car. The magic had gone out of the evening now, and the air on the cliff-face was suddenly cold. I turned round, of course, and looked back when I got to the top, but she was no longer in sight.

I was glad to get into the car, and that, with me, is always a sign that summer is really over. I wondered how much longer I could keep the boat out. With a small boat on a good mooring, getting it in and out for the season is really much more a matter of comfort and inclination than of climatic necessity, especially in these parts, where

70

it can blow hard off and on almost all the year round. You get the boat in in the autumn not primarily because you are thinking of the winter gales, but because the colder and wetter it gets, the less likely you are to want to use it. And of course, with a wooden boat in particular, the longer she is in the water, the more the wear and tear, and the more work you have to do on her while she is laid up. But if you have any good reason for keeping her out, there is no firm deadline. I thought I had a reason. I could not make it sound very reasonable, even to myself, but I had the feeling that I wanted to keep all the approaches to Camlet open, and in fair conditions the sea approach was much more open than the single narrow road winding in on the landward side. So far as wear and tear went, I had nothing to worry about, because the boat had been only two months in the water. If it blew hard, when it blew hard, I would not sail her anyhow. I am unashamedly a fair-weather sailor, because I have a healthy respect for the sea. But I did not think she would come to any harm on her moorings just yet, and if I did need to use her, and the weather made it possible, there she would be.

I did not at the moment see any reason why I should want to go to Camlet. I hoped I should not, because it was my part to be at Letty's call if she needed me, and I did not think she would call me to Camlet unless her need was very urgent indeed. The fact remained that I wanted to be able to go there if I had to, and the sea approach was less easily blocked. In this I was reckoning without Barlow's boat—I assumed that it would be Barlow, if anyone, who would do the blocking—but then I still did not know for certain that he had one. It was one of the things I was always meaning to ask Letty and always forgot to ask her.

I had not been in the house ten minutes when the phone went. I was so certain it was Letty this time that I picked up the receiver and said, "Peter speaking."

She said, "Peter, I'm worried. Derek still isn't back."

"From the island?"

"No, he must be back from the island. The tide's been over the causeway some time. I suppose he might have come back when I was out. But I haven't seen him."

I said, "He could still be there. He could simply have missed the ebb."

"He could, of course. But it's very unlikely. I've never known him do it."

"Well, look," I said, "give him half an hour, and if he still isn't back, ring me again. That's if you want to. If I don't hear, I shall assume all's well, one way or another. At least, I shall assume he's shown up."

She said, "Yes, all right. Bless you, Peter."

I said, "Bless me for nothing. I love you, Letty," and put the receiver down to save her the trouble of answering.

This was all very fine and large, but when I began to think about it, I did not like some of the possible implications. I thought if Barlow had come back from the island and found his wife out, it might have occurred to him to wonder where she was. I did not know he would, of course. From the way she had spoken, I had gathered that Maulness Point was a regular walk of hers. I thought she would be a person who went for solitary walks. Indeed, in that place what else was there for her to do? And she had said he trusted her absolutely. I was not altogether happy about it, all the same.

I watched the half-hour out on the clock, but the phone did not ring again that night.

Chapter Eight

For a whole week after that I heard nothing, and it was not easy to bear, especially when I did not know what had happened to Barlow on the evening Letty and I had met on Maulness Point. I imagined different things at different times, none of them very cheerful. Then in between I told myself it was nonsense. Unless Barlow had her under actual physical restraint, she could have got through to me somehow, and I really had no reason to suppose he would do that. Things clearly had not got to that pitch between them. I did worry over the fact that I could be reached for the most part only in the evenings, and I did not see why Barlow should be out in the evenings now. The evenings were getting very short, and our spell of golden weather had ended in grey skies and westerly winds, so that darkness came earlier than it need have done. What had been the evening ebb was now well into the night. I knew from experience that Barlow could get to the island during the night if he had to, but I did not see why he should with a morning ebb at his disposal, and during the mornings I was seldom at home. I even began, with that perpetual consciousness of the tides you have when you get into the way of it, to try to plan my day so that I should be at home during the time of full ebb, but I could not manage this often if I was to do my work properly. I did manage it once or twice, but the phone never rang. I got my phone calls as usual, in the evenings, but I did not expect any of them to be from Letty, and they were not.

Towards the end of the week I got one phone call I was glad of, and that was from Bill at Canty Port. I had not telephoned the Marlings when I got back from my trip there, because that would be to make too much of an adventure of it, which I would not have. Bill said, "Pete? How are you? We assumed you'd got home all right. There was no report in the local press of the body of a well-dressed man being washed up anywhere."

I took this as a reference to my sailing clothes, and passed it over in silence. I did not always get home by wading through the mud. I left the pram on my moorings, like everybody else, and came home by water. I said, "I'm fine. How are you both? Still occasionally sober?"

"Only when we can't help it," he said. "Look, I thought you might be interested. I did a bit of mild research on your Barlows. It's the same people, all right. A place called Camlet, near Carnholm. That's where they always were. I looked him up, too." Bill always knew where to look things up. He was a bank man, and I suppose it was part of his job. "Commander, R.N., Retired. Does he call himself Commander? I can't remember."

I thought for a moment and then remembered Mr. McAdam. Mr. Barlow, he had called him. "No," I said, "not locally, anyhow. And it's not in the phone book."

"No, well, commanders don't always. Captains always, I think. Anyhow, he retired some years back, in the early sixties, I think, I mean years, not age. It's a naval family, by the look of it. There was an admiral who was probably the father, and what looks like an elder brother, also R.N.

retired. All very solid and respectable, by the look of it."

I said, "Yes, well, I had no reason to doubt their respectability. They looked after me very well and, leaving out any embellishments which may have crept into my narrative, he was really very helpful and very expert."

Bill said, "Yes, only no one seems to know why they suddenly withdrew into their shell like that. I mean, he didn't get arrested, or go bankrupt, or anything. He just opted out."

"Oh well," I said, "that's his business, presumably."

"Oh, no doubt. And Susie said I was to tell you that the wife was quite something, and don't you go pretending she wasn't. I think she suspects you of holding out on her. It's probably just jealousy. You know her hopeless passion for you."

I said, "Why hopeless? Tell her chance her arm some time when you're not around."

"I'll tell her," he said. "But I warn you I'll sue you for alienation of affection. Worth thousands, Susie is, if I handle my case right."

"I'll plead connivance," I said. "Say you threw her into my arms. Well, anyway, Bill, thank you for ringing. It's always nice to know that my rescuers were respectable, even if I had had no real reason to doubt it. See you some time, I hope. Why don't you come over one evening and have a bachelor's meal with me?"

"Oh, nonsense, Susie enjoys cooking, and I bet she does it better than you do. Come over some time properly dressed and in the car. You haven't still got the boat out, have you?"

"Yes, in fact, but mostly because I haven't found time to get her in. Anyway, I promise I'll come by road next time."

"You do that," he said. "Give us a ring and name your day. If it doesn't suit us, we'll find one that will."

I thanked him again, and he rang off. I thought, poor Susie. I wondered what she was really worth to Bill. And then I thought it was silly to be sorry for her, because she was almost certainly perfectly happy in her own way. Not everyone wants to be taken seriously, or too seriously, anyhow. It must make life a lot easier not to be. But mainly I wondered why Bill had gone to all that trouble over the Barlows, and then rung me up expressly to tell me. It was not just that he, or even Susie, was interested in the social phenomenon. I thought their interest was related to me, or why bother to ring up and tell me what he had found out? I wondered just how revealing my behaviour had been that evening, and what I had really said. I could remember very little of what I had said in detail. I just remembered making a good story of my shipwreck and rescue, and retained a general impression of having been the life and soul of the party. I thought all too probably it was what I had not said. I had probably given a full-scale caricature of Barlow, sun-burn and blue eyes and naval silence and all, and said next to nothing about Letty. I remembered the way Susie and I, after years of mild flirtation and public pecks, had suddenly clung to each other like lovers, and my feeling, even then, that it was not Susie I wanted and that Susie knew that perfectly well. It was not, by a long chalk, the first time we had been mildly drunk together, and we had never behaved like that. Perhaps I had Letty written all over me, and Bill, in his friendly, sensible way, had thought it better to fire a warning shot across my bows.

All the same, I was glad he had told me. Once again, the facts fitted, but I could not see what they added up to. Barlow had retired from the Navy at a not unreasonable age for a man with money of his own (if I was right about that), and soon afterwards they would have settled at Camlet. Twelve years ago, Letty had said. For some years they had lived the normal life of their age and social class and then, four or five years ago (this from Susie, but she was probably reliable about things like that) they had suddenly opted out. That would be when the thing, whatever it was, which was now bedevilling their lives had begun. All this added nothing to what little I knew of the thing itself, but it filled in the background and gave depth to the picture. And the fact that Letty had been an admired social figure only added pathos to the tense, silent Letty who took solitary walks to Maulness Point. She would not be a woman to set great store by social success, but she had, evidently, a capacity for ordinary enjoyment which must now be nearly atrophied for want of use. It was not a picture calculated to make me feel any better about her. She had been christened Laetitia, after all, and I was convinced that, given the chance, happiness was natural to her.

At the week-end I decided I could stand the silence no longer. I had to know what was happening. I had told Letty that if I did not hear from her, I might take the law into my own hands. She had begged me not to, but it was impossible to tell whether this still stood. The possibility remained that she would have got in touch with me if she could, but had been prevented. At any rate, these were the arguments I urged in my own justification. I suppose the truth is that I simply could not bear her silence any longer.

I had never yet gone to Camlet by land. The nearest I had got was Clauchrie, two miles west of it. On the map there was a twisting loop of minor road which left the main Carnholm road west of Clauchrie and rejoined it

east of Camlet. The loop threw off small spurs at various
points to serve farms south of it, near the sea, and north
of it, between the loop and the main road. These spurs
would be virtually private roads, even if they were maintained at the public expense. They did not necessarily run
all their length through the land belonging to the farms
they served, but traffic to and from the farms was the only
traffic on them. For obvious reasons, I had been on many
such. The thing you had to remember when using them
was that the farm people, whatever the legal rights of it,
used them as if they were private roads, and drove ac-
cordingly. I had had several near misses already. Where
they left the road, these spurs were always signposted
with the names of the farms they served, as if they were
in fact private drives. I did not know how much land the
Barlows still had with Camlet, or where it began, but I assumed that their spur road, when I came to it, would be
marked, as was the Clauchrie spur which, coming from
my side, I had to pass first. In fact it was not, and I
missed it the first two times, first from one side and then
from the other. The first time I drove right round the loop
and found myself on the Carnholm road again. I turned
and went back, and found myself at the Clauchrie sign
before I realised that I must again have missed the Camlet turning. I knew then that it must be unmarked. I wondered if Barlow had removed the sign, and when. It
would go with what I was beginning to see as an almost
paranoiac wish for seclusion. I got the map out again,
measured the distance between the two spurs, made it a
mile and a half, took the reading on my milometer, turned
the car and set off again.

I found the turning this time because I knew to a very
small distance where it must be. It was not only totally
unmarked, it was next to invisible. It dived off suddenly,

at a very narrow angle to the road, between dry-stone
walls with mixed woodlands, very thick and unkempt,
growing behind them. It did not look as if it went anywhere. I turned and headed cautiously into it, feeling like
Childe Rowland homing in on the dark tower. And I had
lost nearly half an hour in the process. I minded about
this, because I had meant to get to Camlet at the full ebb,
when the causeway would have been uncovered a certain
time and would stay uncovered for an equal time longer.
To say I had a plan was to flatter me, but obviously that
was the time when Barlow, if he went to the island on
this ebb, would be most likely to be there. I had thought
that once he was there, it would be easy, from Camlet, to
see him leave the island on his way back, and I should
have plenty of time to get away before he had negotiated
the causeway. With my half-hour lost, I could not be sure
where he was. I went on cautiously until the narrow rib-
bon of tarmac dipped suddenly, and I saw the sea ahead,
with the roof of the house showing against it above
the tops of the trees. Then, against my original intention,
I stopped suddenly at a field-gate on the left of the track.

There were fields on both sides now. They looked
roughly grazed, but not really in hand. I thought that
they were probably Camlet land, and that Barlow let the
keep for what it would fetch to prevent them from becoming totally over-grown. The gate was rusty, but it
opened. I edged the car through it, bumped a few yards
over the uneven surface until the car was under the wall
and then stopped it and got out. Like that, the car was
not fully concealed from anyone using the spur, but it
would be easy to miss, and at least it was not in the way.
I went out of the field, shut the gate behind me and set
off walking along the spur towards the house. I felt extraordinarily exposed, but this was nonsense, because I

was obviously much less visible than the car would have been. On the other hand, Barlow had never seen my car, and he had certainly seen me. The odds were incalculable anyway. I went on, hoping for the best.

The track continued to drop steadily towards the sea, but the land rose on both sides of it. I could see now, what I had vaguely noticed before, that the house stood in a dip in the coastline, with the cliffs rising on both sides of it. I could see the top of the house on one side of the dip and the top of the island on the other, but between me and them the fields gave way to woodlands again, not big woodlands as close to the sea as that, but tangled stuff which I knew grew right down to the beach and shut in the house itself on all but the seaward side. The woodlands filled the bottom of the dip, but above them on both sides the cliffs rose in bare turf with outcrops of rock where the thin soil could not keep its hold on the craggy skeleton of the land.

When I was perhaps a couple of hundred yards from the house and the beach, I made a fresh decision. I turned off the track left-handed, climbed the dry-stone wall of the last remaining field on that side and started across the field towards the belt of woodland that on its seaward side fringed the beach opposite the island. Time was so short now that I thought it better to make sure of Barlow if he was on the island. The best I could do was to watch the island from the cover of the greenery, and then, the moment he appeared, run to the house in the hope of seeing Letty for at least a few minutes while he was crossing the causeway. As soon as he got near the beach, I could get back into the cover of the trees and find my way back to the car without any fear of his seeing me. If he did not appear by the time the sea was up to the causeway, I should have to assume that he was already in or near the house, and then I could think again. The only thing I did not want was to come on him unexpectedly. I jog-trotted across the rest of the field, climbed over another dry-stone wall and plunged into the green tangle on the other side.

As so often with neglected and overgrown woodlands, it was much less impenetrable, at least at ground level, than it looked from the outside. The trees grew so thickly overhead that the undergrowth was stunted and patchy. I dodged about a bit to avoid the worst obstacles, but on the whole I thought I was holding to a fairly direct line, and I made surprisingly good going. It was only at the last that I ran into really thick stuff, where the sunlight and rain from the seaward side gave it a chance to grow, but this did not last long. In another minute I could see light through chinks in the wall of greenery, and then suddenly I stopped, with only a screen of bushes between me and the final drop to the beach.

Right opposite me, a dark green hump under the grey sky, the island sat on its footing of black rocks. The sea, as grey as the sky and rumpled by the steady wind, was already well round both sides of it, breaking on the mud in a small scurry of surf as it advanced. Between me and the island, and between the two advancing lines of sea, a stretch of mud, perhaps forty yards wide at its widest, ran straight out from the beach. It was narrower in the middle, because the water came in quicker over the lower ground, but there was not much in it. This was the picture which Barlow, the only time I had been here, had not allowed me to see. I had only to wait to see the exact line of the central causeway itself, but I could see already that its landward end would be a little west of where I now stood. I dodged back into the bushes, went about thirty yards westwards and then tried again. This was it. I

81

was now exactly opposite the central line of the remaining stretch of mud, and I could see from here the slight spine of higher ground which no doubt marked the hidden rock ridge which made the causeway. I took out my knife and cut a good-sized blaze on the trunk of the nearest tree. When I looked round again, Barlow was leaving the island beach and starting along the causeway on his way home.

This should have been the signal for me to run to the house. I did not, because almost as soon as I saw him, I realised that there was something odd in the way he was moving. His usually powerful stride seemed uncertain, and then, as I looked at him out of my screen of bushes, he wavered and stopped for a moment, as if he was uncertain of his bearings. I could not understand this. The line in front of him must be as clear to him as it was to me, and still he looked unsure of himself. Then he came on again, and as he got nearer it occurred to me suddenly that the trouble was not in the ground under his feet, but in the man himself. He was definitely unsteady now, still coming forward, but in a weaving, uncertain line, so that I wondered for a moment if he was drunk. When he was no more than twenty yards from the beach, he stopped again, and this time his hands went to his head, as if he was dizzy or in pain. Then he came on again, but there was an almost desperate effort in every stride, and I could see, even in that grey light, that his usually florid face was ashy pale. He had reached the bottom of the beach now, and there he stopped again, hardly more than fifteen yards from me. He straightened his great shoulders and threw his head back, and for a moment a grin of satisfaction took his lips back in a sort of horrifying rictus. Still with that ghastly smile on his face, he came a few yards up the beach, turned left as if to head for the house and hesitated again. Then his knees went from under him, and he collapsed, first on all fours and then face-down on the pebbles.

My first impulse, in mere humanity, was to go to him, but I knew I must not. He was in no danger. It would be a long time now before the tide reached him, if he was not already clear of the high-water mark. I turned back and fought my way through the tangled stuff of the wood's seaward edge. Once in clearer ground, I turned westwards and ran, if I could call it running, through the wood in the direction of the house. I knew it could not be far to the road, and I came to it sooner than I expected. I ran, as fast as I could run now, down the rest of the road, through the stone gateposts and up the drive of the house, and as I ran I shouted for Letty Barlow.

Chapter Nine

She opened the door as I came to it. I said, "Derek's hurt. He's down on the beach, this end of the causeway. Can you come?"

She said, "Hurt how? What happened?" When I came to think of it afterwards, it seemed to me that she had not at any point asked a single unnecessary question. I thought I had never loved or admired her more than I had during those few minutes when she had no thought to give to me at all.

"I don't know," I said. "I think he's hurt his head. I saw him coming across, and he was groggy then."

"Did he see you?"

"No."

"What's he doing?"

"When I saw him last, lying down. But he may have come round by now."

"You didn't go to him?"

"I thought better not."

"What about the tide?"

"It won't reach him for hours. Maybe not at all, but I'm not sure." That was true, too. I knew the local tides by now. They come in over the mud-flats so fast that you think you must have got the time of high water wrong,

84

and then they take hours creeping inch by inch up the steep beach above the mud. And Barlow had been well up the beach before he fell.

She said, "Wait a moment," and turned and went up the stairs two at a time. It is a strange experience for the ordinary man, and a little unnerving, to see a graceful woman suddenly transformed into a tigress, especially if he happens to love her, and it is not himself she is being tigerish about. She came down almost as fast with a couple of blankets and a pillow. I wondered if there was nursing experience there. Perhaps just first-aid training, but if so, it had stuck more than it does with most people. "Come on, then," she said.

We ran down the drive and down the rest of the road until it came out on to the beach. Then she said, "I think you'd better wait here while I go to him. If he has come round, he'd better not see you. What do you think?"

It was the first time she had asked for my advice, and I gave it. I said, "I'll wait here. If he's on his feet, get him back to the house, and I'll keep out of sight. If he's still down, make him comfortable and then come back. Leave him face down, it's the best way he can lie, only make sure he can breathe." I thought for a man with concussion, which was what it looked like, a pebble beach was safer than a pillow, but I did not say so. I thought very probably she knew it too, but she did not say so either.

She just nodded. "Right," she said, and was off along the beach. I watched her until she was out of sight. The beach curved a little, and from here the place where Barlow was lying was just, but I thought only just, hidden by the bottom of the sea bank, waiting to see what would emerge, and ready to dodge back if it included Barlow on his feet. I felt useless and a little foolish, but I knew that this was not really reasonable. They also serve who only

85

stand and wait. I might yet prove, for all I knew, to have saved Barlow's life with my rather silly scouting. Seeing what I felt about his wife, I hoped this might be counted to me for righteousness. I did not see what else I was likely to get out of it. Perhaps I was still a little bit awed by the tigress.

I waited for what was probably only three or four minutes, though it felt longer. Then Letty appeared by herself. She was hurrying, not running, because it is a doubtful expediency to try to run along a steep pebble beach, but making the best speed she could. I stepped out of my unnecessary hiding and went to meet her. I waited for her to speak. I was not asking any unnecessary questions either.

"I think he's all right," she said. "He's had a bang on the head, I think, but it doesn't feel a bad one, and the skin's not broken. He'll be a bit concussed, but he's all right for the moment. I'm going to phone the doctor." She said the doctor, not a doctor. I was glad to know they still had one. Then she said, "I'd better get an ambulance, too. We'll need a stretcher party if he's still out."

We hurried back to the house. I think at first we broke into a trot on the road, but the gradient was steep and we were soon walking again. Even walking it was as much as I could do to keep up with her. I thought it was not only gaiety that had been suppressed in her all these years, it was energy too, mental and physical. When we got to the house, she went in to telephone and I waited by the door. I do not know why I did not go in with her, except that for the moment I felt something of an outsider. Then she came out and said, "Coming. About twenty minutes with any luck. The ambulance, anyhow." Then all of a sudden there was nothing more we could do, and we stood there looking at each other. For the first and last time, I felt something like embarrassment in her presence. But she put out a hand suddenly and took mine, as she had that evening on Maulness Point. "Thank you, Peter," she said, and the tigress was no longer there, or if it was, it was a tigress under control and I felt, for the first time, perhaps even a little mine.

Then she took her hand away, and I said, "I don't think there's anything more I can do, is there? Had I better be going?"

She thought for a moment. "Where's your car?" she said. "You're not blocking the road, are you?"

"No, but it is just visible from the road, and it might strike anybody as an odd place to leave it."

"The ambulance men wouldn't notice it," she said, "and it wouldn't matter if they did. Dr. Reid might, though."

I said, "If I go at once, I can get it out on to the main road before anyone arrives. Shall I do that?"

"I think it would be better. I'll phone you, or if I can't phone, I'll write. Thank you again, Peter."

I made what was perhaps a rather hopeless gesture. I did not really want her to thank me, because I did not want her to feel too grateful to me for rescuing her husband, if I had rescued him. I knew it was not very noble, but that was what I felt. For the matter of that, he and I had rescued each other now, and I doubt if either of us had done it with a very full heart. She was looking at me, but I still could not find anything to say, and time was short, so I just turned and went off down the drive.

I hurried back to the car, listening all the time for the ambulance ahead of me on the road and ready to dodge out of its way, and if possible out of sight, if it did come. But there was plenty of the twenty minutes left, and not even the most efficient ambulance service often arrives before its promised time. It was when I got to the car that the thing became acute. Once I had the car on the spur road, there was no dodging anything. I backed the car in the field, ran it out on to the road, pulled the gate roughly shut and drove with a sort of cautious desperation for the loop road. I made it. I still do not know with how much to spare, but I made it. When I got to the road, I turned left. That was in any case my way home, and the ambulance at least would be coming from Carnholm, and probably the doctor too. But once I was on the loop road, it did not matter, after all. I might just be looking for Mr. McAdam at Clauchrie. So I drove on quietly, and now for the first time I really thought about what had happened.

It was Letty Barlow I thought about first. I spent a good deal of my time thinking about her these days, and now I had a lot more to think about. Of all the questions she had asked me, she had never asked the one question which almost any other woman in the world would have had to ask. She had never asked me what I was doing there at all. I tried to read all sorts of implications into this, but I thought the truth probably was that she had not asked because at the time it had not really mattered. From this my mind moved to the fact that, however admirable her reaction to the emergency, she had never, so far as I could tell, shown any sign of being particularly surprised. Her whole reaction had had something in it of the reaction of the casualty sister at a hospital, even of the air raid warden, who reacts quickly and efficiently to an emergency largely because an emergency is not unexpected, or at least is always possible. She had asked me, at first, what had happened, but I thought that was mainly to establish my part in it. Once she knew that I had not been directly involved, she had not taken the thing any further. I wondered if part at least of her worry about her husband and his visits to the island had not been precisely the anticipation that an accident of this sort, whatever it was, might at some time happen. If this was so, it was, so far as I was concerned, an entirely new element in the situation. I had thought that she was worried by Barlow's obsession with the island, if that was what it was, and its effect on him and indirectly on herself. The idea that the obsession involved actual danger to him had not occurred to me. Or perhaps up to now it had not involved it, but she had seen it coming if the thing went on, and this had been one of her reasons for breaking down and telling me about it. In any case, I had the feeling that Barlow's mishap, however it had happened, might have the effect of speeding up the whole process. In this at least I was right. From what I know now, I think it probable that what had happened that day was in some sense the first step towards the final catastrophe.

In a curious way, this new idea was a relief to me. In the days that followed I think I worried less about Letty Barlow than I had before. It was, after all, Letty I was concerned with. Barlow himself meant very little to me. I had seen next to nothing of him, and even then I had found him impenetrable and unsympathetic. If he was in danger, it seemed to be a danger he had brought on himself, and I judged him more than capable of dealing with it. As far as I could tell, the danger did not extend to his wife. I felt for her in her worry over him, but I could live more easily with the idea of physical danger to him, even if it involved worry for her, than I could with the undefined menace which had seemed to hang over them both. Perhaps, again, that was not very noble of me, but perhaps I am not a very noble person. At any rate, in the ignoble part of my mind I thought that if Barlow destroyed himself by whatever he was doing, at least it would end her long distress, and then she might turn to me. And I wanted her now more than I had ever wanted anything.

The only practical effect of the thing, so far as I was concerned, was nearly a week's silence, but now I was better able to bear it. As I have said, I was worrying less about Letty herself, and in any case I assumed that Barlow had had his wings clipped for the moment and would not be returning to the island just yet. That in itself could account for her failure to telephone. I did not really expect her to write, except perhaps to ask me to meet her. It is much more difficult not to say things in a letter than it is on the telephone, and I knew there was still a great deal that she was not saying. Finally, it was a fact that I had worried myself sick over not hearing from her the week before, and I had found her safe and sound, without even any explanation of why she had not phoned. The truth probably was that I had abrogated the original agreement, at least mentally, on my side, and she had not. To her, I was still there on the sidelines, ready to be called in if needed. For myself, I felt fully involved, with her and with her troubles, and to be away from her was in itself a conscious frustration and loss. But I could see that in fact the change was one-sided. My job was still to be there if needed, and I had to accept it.

And then towards the end of the week she telephoned. It was early in the evening, and I had only just got in. It occurred to me, even as I heard her voice at the other end, that the tide should just be off the causeway now, and I wondered if Barlow was back on his old routine. She said, "Peter?"

"Yes," I said. "How's Derek?"

"Oh, he's all right," she said. "It wasn't much, just mild concussion. The doctor told him to stay in bed for several days, and he stayed exactly twenty-four hours." Until the next daylight ebb, I thought, but I did not say so. "He's about again now, and apparently none the worse."

"What happened?" I said. I knew it was a question she would not welcome, but it was such an obvious one in the circumstances that it would have seemed palpably disingenuous not to ask it.

She said, "He said he slipped and fell on the rocks as he came down on to the beach. On the island, I mean. He was wearing gumboots, and of course they can be a menace if they're wet." She said it in a completely flat tone, as if she was simply reporting Barlow's explanation without offering any comment on it.

"Well," I said, "so long as he's all right." I did not suppose that she believed it any more than I did. He had been wearing gumboots, certainly, but he had presumably been on the island some time, and it was a dry day. They could not have been still wet when he came down the path on his way home. And a conscious man, with his feet on the ground, very seldom hits his head when he falls. The instinct to protect it is too strong. It is one of the standard explanations for head injuries, but it is very seldom true. But even assuming that Letty disbelieved the story of a fall as much as I did, that still did not mean that she knew the truth, or at any rate the whole truth. If, as I had thought, she had been half expecting something of the sort to happen, she certainly knew a great deal more than I did. But she had said she did not know the whole of it, and I believed her.

She had said nothing for some time. I said, "Letty?"

"Yes," she said, "yes, I'm still here." There was suddenly the same hopelessness and desolation in her voice as I had heard before, and there seemed to be nothing I could do for her, and that made it worse.

I said, "Letty, can't we meet one of these evenings? If

you're free." I meant if Barlow was back on the island again on the evening ebb.

But she said, "Oh, Peter, what's the use?" and I could not tell what use it would be, because I did not know myself. I knew that I wanted to see her, and I believed now that she wanted to see me, but I did not really suppose that it would make either of us any happier.

"All right," I said, "if you'd rather not," but she whipped the words out of my mouth with a fierceness that took my breath away.

"Oh don't be a fool," she said, "of course I want to see you. But it can't do any good, and it could do a lot of harm, and we ought to have more sense."

My mouth was dry and I felt my heart thudding as if it was bumping about in an enormous cavity. But she had given so much away so suddenly that I could afford to take things calmly now. "It's up to you," I said. "You know that. I can't make any sort of a decision. I haven't enough to go on. Tell me what you want, and I'll do it."

"Just be there," she said. "Please just be there for a bit, Peter. Do you mind?"

"It doesn't seem much," I said, "but if it helps—"

She said, "It keeps me sane."

"All right, Letty," I said, "I'll be here."

She said, "Thank you, Peter," and put the receiver down. I put mine down slowly, but the moment it was down the bell rang again and I whipped it up. But it was only Mr. McAdam.

"I've been trying to get you," he said, "but the line's been engaged."

I said, "Oh, good evening, Mr. McAdam. I'm so sorry. I've had a lot on hand and that's a fact."

"Ay, well," he said, "I expect we keep you busy between us. There was just the one thing I wanted to ask."

We plunged into the technicalities of my trade. But all the time, in my mind, I was just being there, keeping Letty Barlow sane.

Chapter Ten

It was only a few days later that Barlow did his best to kill me. I should say at once that there was nothing personal in it, not at that stage. It might have been anyone he was trying to kill, only it just happened to be me. I had been in Carnholm, and had decided to start my return journey by the loop road and call and see Mr. McAdam on the way. He was still my biggest single customer, and I knew that one customer satisfied on this scale could be of incalculable value to me. That was why I was still giving him five-star treatment. The fact that he lived so close to Camlet caused me as much misery as it did excitement. I still think Mr. McAdam was treated strictly on his commercial merits.

As I drove round the loop from east to west, I had of course to pass the Camlet spur before I came to Clauchrie. It emerged from its trees and joined the loop road at a very acute angle, so that anyone coming from Camlet and turning east, towards Carnholm, would have to come virtually to a halt and make a hairpin turn, whereas anyone turning west could filter straight out on to the road, subject always to the possibility of other traffic coming pretty well from behind him on his side of the road. I looked for the Camlet turning, of course, as I came up to it, partly because it was so invisible that I could still not be sure of it, and partly I suppose because I hoped to see a green Renault Six waiting to turn out of it. Anyhow, whatever made me look for it, it must have been the saving of me. Just before I came to the junction I got a glimpse through the trees of something moving faster than I was and on a collision course. I braked and swung the wheel hard to the right a split second before it came in on my left, and the next moment my car and a big saloon were careering along side by side, with no more than inches between them, and filling the narrow road almost completely. Mercifully there was nothing coming from the opposite direction.

I do not know how long this lasted, probably not as long as it seemed. We were both braking, of course, and both losing speed at much the same rate, so that we stayed side by side. If one of us had had the wit to accelerate while the other braked, we could have got clear of each other, but the instinct to stop the car if you can is very strong, and neither of us thought of it. Finally we bumped, not seriously, but quite unmistakably, and the next moment I had two wheels on the grass verge on my side of the road and was bouncing madly to a halt with my right wing only inches from a dry-stone wall. The other car stayed on the road—it was bigger than I was, and had had the better of the clash—ran on another twenty yards or so and came to a halt still on the tarmac. We both cut our engines and the silence was suddenly absolute. I sat there with my knees vibrating gently under the steering wheel, and then Barlow got out of the car ahead and walked back towards me along the narrow road. I watched him come for a moment or two, and then climbed out of my car to meet him.

The look on his face as he started back was exactly

what you might expect of him in the circumstances. It
was the look of a man who knew he had been in the
wrong, but was determined to put the best face on it he
could. He looked unruffled, prepared even to be slightly
amused by the whole thing if he could persuade the other
party to share his amusement. His step was slow and
confident, and he was giving nothing away. Then I got
out of my car, and a moment later he recognised me, and
the whole picture changed. I think he even hesitated a
moment in his stride and then came on again, but the
carefully composed pleasantness had gone. He was still in
the wrong, but it was no longer our minor accident which
was in the front of his mind. He said, "What are you
doing here?"

He said it exactly as he had that first time on the island,
with his torch flood-lighting me as I sat on the heather
with the foresail wrapped round my legs. It was not
directly hostile, but he wanted to know and expected an
answer. Only the difference was that there and then he
had had a right to ask it, and here and now he had none.

I said, "Do you always come out on to the road like
that?" I was shaken, of course, more shaken than I was
prepared to admit, and I was angry at what seemed to me
his effrontery. But apart from that, I was trying desperately to adjust my mind to an actual meeting with him
and the assumptions that must underlie what I said and
how I behaved. So far as he knew, I had not seen him or
given him a thought since he had walked up off that small
beach, leaving me mending my boat and waiting for the
tide to come up and take me off the island. In fact, I had
had him constantly in mind almost ever since, I had
talked about him to his wife and to Bill Marling and
above all I had seen him at close quarters during, to put
it at its lowest, a completely unguarded moment. I

viewed him as he came towards me with an almost startling degree of recognition and familiarity, but I must not
let any of this show. I took refuge in an aggressiveness I
did not in fact feel and in a refusal, at least at first, even
to acknowledge our previous meeting.

I thought for a moment he was going to come at me,
and I did not at all like the prospect. I had been in some
queer places in my younger and unregenerate days, and
reckoned I could fight up to my weight, but I was no more
than a welter-weight at most, and Barlow was well up in
the heavyweight class, and strong with it. But he must
have seen it would not do. Whatever resentment or suspicion he felt against me, he could not admit it. His behaviour was bounded by the facts of our present encounter, and on those facts he was in the wrong. The sudden,
alarming anger went out of his face and something of his
previous quizzical assurance returned to it. He said,
"Sorry if I came out a bit fast. There was nothing on the
road ahead, and I thought there'd be room for everybody. Have I marked you at all?"

His effrontery remained breath-taking, but I had no
wish to quarrel with him over a matter which was, to me,
the least important thing about him. The whole interview
took place, certainly on my side and I am fairly certain on
his, against a huge and lowering background of *arrière-
pensée* which reduced the interview itself to the sig-
nificance of a puppet-show. We turned and went to
look at the near side of my car as she stood half on and
half off the green verge of the road. There was very little
to show, in fact. A slight dent leading into a slight
scratch, but she was far from unmarked already. I said,
"Nothing of any importance. I must say, you startled me,
coming out like that, but we nearly managed to miss each
other." Then I remembered his previous question. As it

happened, it was one I could answer in good faith, and in that conversation the opportunity was not to be missed. "I'm on my way to see Mr. McAdam at Clauchrie," I said. "Do you know him?"

"McAdam?" he said. "I've met him, of course. I can't say I see much of him. What takes you there?"

I told him, and he showed a reasonable degree of polite interest. "I see," he said. "I didn't know what you did in the intervals of navigation." He turned and looked at me suddenly. He said, "You got to Canty Port all right at your second attempt? You seemed well on your way when I saw you."

I smiled pleasantly. The puppet-show had suddenly become the real thing. "Oh, yes, thank you," I said, "no trouble that time. I didn't know you'd seen me. When was that?"

"Well," he said, "you stood in towards the western side of the island, and I thought for a moment you were going to come in and visit us. Then you suddenly wore round and stood out again, so I imagined you'd thought better of it."

Something in the words he used set an alarm bell ringing in my mind, so that I did not say what I had been just going to say. I think it was his saying us, visit us, but I am not sure why. I said, "Where were you, then?"

"Oh," he said, "at one of our top back windows. They command a good view seawards, and we don't see much moving as a rule. So when I saw your sail, of course I got the glass on you, and then I saw who it was."

"Well, to tell you the truth," I said, "I wanted to see how I'd managed to make a very odd mistake I made the first time. I know this sounds pretty silly, but the truth is, when I came ashore on your island, I didn't know it was an island. I thought it was just a small headland. Not that

I had any choice, of course, but I did think that. It wasn't until I'd walked up to the top and seen the sea between me and the mainland that I realised what I'd done. And then, of course, I went too far and assumed it was permanently cut off instead of tidal. Anyway, the next time I did the trip I was watching it, and I found that in fact from out at sea you don't see it as an island unless you know it is one. You have to stand quite a long way in before you can see it like that. That's why I came in as I did. As soon as I'd seen what I wanted to see, I stood out again. And of course you're quite right, I was well in sight of the house by then. But I didn't know you'd sighted me."

He said, "Ah, that was it. I wondered, of course. Anyway, you got to Canty Port all right and found your way home again?"

"Yes, thank you. No trouble." I had already assured him of this once, but now the puppets were on stage again.

"Good," he said. "Now about your car. Suppose I give you a fiver to get that dent knocked out, and we call it quits? I'm certainly not bringing in my insurance people, and I don't imagine you are."

The temptation to wave aside his offer was powerful and immediate, but I knew it must be resisted. I myself might feel that I would not touch a penny of Barlow's money, but as puppet to puppet the offer was a perfectly reasonable one, and to refuse it would in itself be suspect. "All right," I said, "that's fair enough. I'm bound to say I think it was your fault, but I'll be glad to settle the thing on that basis if you will."

One puppet grinned and bobbed at the other puppet, and the second puppet got out a five-pound note and gave it to the first puppet, and all the pair of them had to do then was to get themselves decently off stage. "Well," he said, "I'll be getting on, then, as I'm already ahead of you. Nice to have seen you again." He made a gesture of good-bye and turned and was off to his car. I watched him for a moment and then turned and went back to mine.

And nice to have seen you, Mr. Barlow, I thought. We seemed to have been seeing quite a bit of each other, one way and another, though mostly through field-glasses, which so far as I was concerned was close enough. I eased the car off the grass and drove on to Clauchrie, where I had a nice, simple, one-tier conversation with Mr. Mc-Adam.

All the same, it was left to Mr. McAdam to provide the biggest surprise of the day, though not until I had got home for the evening. He rang up and asked some fairly trifling question about our earlier conversation, so trifling that I wondered for a moment, valuable as he was to me, whether he might not prove too much of a good thing, and have at some point to be choked off a little. However, I answered his question with a proper patience, and then he paused for a moment and said, "I had your friend Mr. Barlow, him at Camlet, round this evening. You'll not have known him long, maybe?"

For a moment I hesitated, but only for a moment, because there was no mistaking Mr. McAdam's tone, or even, now, his reason for ringing me up at all. He did not like Barlow, and to that extent I could trust him. "Mr. Barlow?" I said. "No, indeed. I'd only met him once before today, and then today I nearly ran into him in my car, or he into me, in fact. Why, Mr. McAdam? Did he mention me?"

He was silent for a moment. I could picture him sucking his teeth, as he did when he was hesitating to take a decision. Then he said, "Ay, he did that. Well, not to say mention you—he was more asking questions about you."

I had all I wanted now. I was grateful to Mr. McAdam, but clearly the less made of it, the better. "Oh well," I said, "I expect it was because of our accident. As I say, we had just about met before, but he knew nothing about me. And the truth is, the thing was his fault. It was a lunatic bit of driving, and he knew it. We parted on fair terms, but I expect he was worried I might take the thing further, and wanted to know more about me."

Mr. McAdam did not want to be pacified, but he could hardly be indignant on my behalf if I was not prepared to be on my own. "That's as may be," he said, "but why would he come to me?"

"That's easy," I said. "Because I told him I was on my way to you when we had our accident. So he knew you knew me, and you were a neighbour of his, so naturally he asked you about me. Anyhow," I said, "please don't let it worry you, Mr. McAdam. It was kind of you to ring, but believe me, it doesn't worry me, so there's no reason why it should worry you."

He accepted this grudgingly, and I thanked him again, and at last he rang off. But of course I knew why Barlow had gone to Clauchrie. He had simply wanted to find out whether I had really gone there and, if so, what my business there was. He wanted to be sure what had brought me into the neighbourhood of Camlet by land, just as he had wanted to be sure what had brought me there by sea. I did not think he had any solid reason for suspecting my interest in his affairs. I was certain he did not connect it in any way with his wife. I thought he just suspected it on principle. The fact remained that he was, or at any rate had been, suspicious of me, and whether or not he had any evidence to support it, his suspicion was in fact well founded. I should have to be very careful indeed.

But for the rest of the week I had nothing to be careful about. I told myself that I was just being there, helping Letty Barlow to keep sane, but I did not find it a very satisfactory role. I think my meeting with Barlow had sharpened my sense of personal antagonism. For some time now I had been seeing him mostly through Letty's eyes, and once, through my own, when he was damaged but making a fight of it, and I had generated, if rather unwillingly, some sort of sympathy for him. Our meeting on the loop road had changed all that. Whatever pressures he was under, he was a man I did not like, and above all did not trust. For all his silence and restraint, there was a lot of violence in him. Even at the simplest level, the way he drove his car showed that. I speculated a lot about his relations with his wife, past and present. I did not enjoy these speculations, but I could not resist them. You cannot, if you are in love with another man's wife, or even with a woman you think prefers someone else. It is like a sore spot in your mouth which you must lick. I knew there was a lot in him which would have appealed to any woman so long as things were going as he wanted them. Now that in some way they were not, his natural egotism seemed to have taken on more than a touch of monomania, and I thought he would be hell to live with. So far as I was concerned, this cut both ways. It made it much more difficult to stand back and leave Letty to deal with him, but it also emphasised the danger to her if I did not. So I went on doing nothing, and hated every moment of it.

When the week-end came, I thought it was time I got the boat in. It was a fortnight since Barlow had been hurt on the island, and we were back to a mid-day ebb and evening flood. The hour or so before high water was the best time to get the boat up the beach and on to its trailer, and now I had two evenings at my disposal. I should need an extra hand or two, but did not doubt that I could recruit that on the spot. Then on the Saturday morning the phone went, and when I picked up the receiver and answered, I heard the insistent whining of a call-box wanting its money. The whining stopped and Letty said, "Peter?"

"Yes," I said, "where are you?"

"Only Carnholm, I'm afraid."

"On your own?"

"Yes, but I haven't got long, and I've got shopping to do. Peter, what happened between you and Derek? He said he'd seen you."

"He nearly ran into me in his car. I was driving to Clauchrie, and he came out of your turning like a lunatic. We only bumped slightly, but it was small thanks to him it wasn't worse."

"Oh," she said, "I know, he does that. What happened then?"

"We stopped. He hadn't known it was me, of course. When he saw who it was, he asked me what I was doing there."

"You told him? I mean—you really were going to Clauchrie?"

"I told him. I was and I did. And later he went round to Clauchrie to check up. And McAdam told him. And then McAdam told me."

"Oh, Peter, I'm sorry."

"It doesn't do me any harm," I said. "It's you I'm worrying about. There was another thing that came up, too. He said he'd seen me sail past the island on a Saturday.

That was a fortnight after my original shipwreck. He wanted to know about that, too."

"And had you?"

"Yes. I told you I'd been going to visit people at Canty Port when I'd run into trouble. I actually did the trip a fortnight later."

"And you told him that, too?"

"Oh yes. Whether he believed me I don't know. On one point at least he lied to me."

"What was that?"

"He told me he'd seen me from the house. In fact I had seen him from the boat, only a glimpse, but it was him, all right. And he wasn't at the house, he was on the island."

There was quite a long silence. Then the coin-box clamoured to be fed, and she must have put another coin in, because it stopped clamouring, but still there was silence at the other end of the line. "Letty?" I said. "Letty, are you still there?"

"Yes," she said, "I'm still here." The words had exactly the same effect they had had the last time I had heard her say them. They seemed to crystallise her desolation, for her and for me.

I said, "Letty, can't I—" but she stopped me.

"No, Peter," she said. "There's nothing you can do. But please be very careful. He mustn't know you're interested in him. Above all, he mustn't know I've talked to you. Promise me, Peter?"

There was, indeed, nothing I could do. I said, "All right, Letty. You know where to find me."

She said, "Yes, all right, Peter," and then she put the receiver down.

The only result of the call was that I did not get the boat in. I cannot explain the connection, or not logically, but there was one. Perhaps Letty's call merely put it out of my head, or at least diverted my attention. But I did not get the boat in that week-end, and that turned out to be very important later.

Chapter Eleven

I had never seen Letty Barlow's handwriting, but I knew it as soon as I saw it. Admittedly a hand-written letter with a local postmark was a rarity. Nearly all my outside correspondence was typed, and local business was invariably conducted on the telephone or face to face. But I did not need that to tell me it was her hand, it was so like her, strong and controlled, but fluent and elegant. I do not go in for heavy psychology, and the so-called graphologists seem to me mostly phonies, but I like writing for its own sake, and of course people write characteristically, just as they speak and eat and drive their cars characteristically. And fine handwriting is a dying art, like letter writing. I remembered that Letty had said she wrote and received letters, too, which in her position was understandable.

Not that there were any graces in the letter itself. Even the formalities were skimped. I thought it had been written in a hurry, though there was no haste in the writing itself. It just said, *"Could you possibly be at Maulness at about ten on Wednesday morning? But don't if you oughtn't to. I'll be there at ten and wait as long as I can."* It was signed just L. I went to my diary. I ought not to, clearly, but equally clearly I was going whether I ought to or not. I should have been seeing a farmer called McConnell—many of the names in these parts are more Irish than Scots—about a new muck-spreader we thought a lot of. But I had already met Mr. McConnell, and had reckoned him a casual sort of chap. Perhaps it was the Irish in him. I got on the phone to him at once and must have caught him at breakfast. He did not seem to mind, and I sold him a story as easily as I hoped to sell him his new muck-spreader. We changed the date, and my whole mind settled down to wait for Wednesday. It would be the morning ebb, of course.

It could not have been less like that first golden evening we had met there. It was grey and drizzly, with a wind puffing from the west. Not yet really cold, but not as warm as it had been, and very cheerless. After all, we were into October. I wore my ordinary working clothes and took gumboots and a mackintosh in the car. Letty Barlow was in the same place when I saw her, wearing a grey mackintosh and a dark red headscarf, a small dark figure against a grey, restless sea. You could not see the English coast at all. We repeated our former movements exactly, and when we met, it must have been within a yard or two of where we had met the first time. Only this time she held out her hands to me, and I took them in mine, and we stood holding both hands and looking at each other. Her headscarf and face were beaded with the rain. Her mouth would be cold and a little wet if I kissed it, but I would not let myself even try. She must come to me of her own accord or not at all. I said, "What's the trouble, Letty?"

She looked at me for a moment or two without speaking, but there was a different quality in her silence. She was not thinking what she wanted to say. She knew what she wanted to say, but could not quite bring herself to say it. Then she shook her head a little, and for a moment her eyes left mine. She said, "I don't think anything new, really. I just wanted to see you. Have I taken you away from anything important?"

I am not much good at pretty speeches, but even to me it did not seem feasible to tell the woman I loved that I rated her higher than a muck-spreader. I just tightened my grip on her hands and shook my head. I said, "Thank you for writing, Letty. I wanted to see you, too. But then I always do."

We still stood there, holding hands and looking at each other, and one of us had to say something. I said, "Why the letter, by the way? Couldn't you phone?"

"Not easily, no. Or not when you'd be at home."

"Not even from Carnholm?"

She hesitated a moment, and then said, "I haven't been there alone."

"Is that something new?"

"I can't tell exactly. I think it may be, yes."

"How did you post your letter, then?"

"That was in Carnholm. I had others to go. I just kept yours in my bag and put it in with the others at the box." She looked away again, and then looked at me with a small, tight-lipped smile. "One soon learns the tricks," she said.

I said, "Like an ordinary, bored wife looking for a flutter?"

She looked up at me with a sort of despairing resignation. "I suppose so, yes," she said.

I said, "Letty—" and then I stopped. I did not know how to go on, because all the lines seemed blocked with clichés. This is different. This is the real thing. There is nothing to be ashamed of in our love. I don't feel that way about you. All the script-writers in the business grinned and shook their heads at me, because they had got in first. I supposed in fact I felt about her just as any other man feels about the woman he has fallen in love with when she happens to be somebody else's wife. Only I had told myself that she was different, and now here she was telling me that she was the same, too. It was the most valuable thing I had, but there did not seem to be anything worth saying about it.

Then I thought to hell with it, so long as there were two of us in it. I smiled at her and said, "Can't we just be commonplace together?" I spread our joined hands and pulled her to me. She let herself come, only she had not smiled in answer to my smile. We let go each other's hands and clung to each other, but she kept her head down, and even as I felt that wonderful, taut body against mine, I knew that this was not a triumph but some sort of capitulation.

She said, "I'm afraid, Peter." There was no whimper in it, nothing of the child wanting comfort and reassurance in the dark room. It was a considered statement, as if she was facing the fact for the first time. Then she raised her head and looked at me, and her eyes were serious and her mouth hard. "Do you understand?" she said. "Nothing noble in it, not any longer. It's not Derek I'm afraid for, it's myself. I'm just plain scared."

"Of Derek?" I said, and she nodded.

"I suppose so, yes." But there seemed a shade of doubt in it.

I said, "Then for God's sake, leave him, Letty." She went on looking at me. "I don't mean run away with me," I said. "I mean pack your things and get into your car and just drive off. Anywhere, a long way from here. There must be people you can go to. Haven't you got a family?"

She shook her head. "Not one I'd choose to run to," she

said. "And apart from anything else, my car's not working."

"Since when?"

"Three days ago, when I wrote to you."

"What's wrong with it?"

"I don't know. It just won't start. I don't know much about cars."

"Does Derek know?"

"Of course," she said. "He keeps saying he'll have a look at it. He knows all about cars. But he doesn't seem to find time for it. He says we can use his, and we do. But I've never driven his, and in any case he's got the keys."

"Can't you just phone a garage?"

"How can I? He's always done everything that's needed to both cars. He wouldn't have a mechanic near the place. Or anyone else, if he can help it." She pulled herself a little away from me and almost shook me in her desperation. "Don't you understand?" she said. "I'd be more frightened if I left him than I am here. You don't know Derek."

"I'm beginning to," I said.

"No," she said, "I'm all right so long as I stay here, and do what he wants, and just go on as usual." Her voice was perfectly steady. She spoke of her fear as if it was something she had to live with, and could if she had to. She had that sort of courage. "And so long as he doesn't know I've been seeing you," she said. "That above all. You know that, don't you?"

I said, "He's suspicious of me. From what you say, he's now suspicious of you. But I don't see that he can possibly have anything to go on."

"He hasn't," she said. "I agree, he can't have. No, he just suspects every one. And it's growing on him all the time. He's—" she checked for a moment and then brought

it out—"he's not right in his head, not really. It began as a
sort of total commitment, then it became an obsession
and now he's all but paranoiac. And he was a sound man
once. Never easy, but sound. But there's an odd streak in
the family. And like that—I don't know what he might do.
Not if things really went wrong."

"For the matter of that," I said, "he's damned near
killed me twice already. But I don't think he had the least
intention of killing me either time."

"Twice? In the car, do you mean?"

"Once in the car. And once, if what you say is right,
when I was on the island. I was going to swim for it, you
know, and you say if I had, I shouldn't have come ashore
alive. But I was going to swim for it only because I didn't
know he'd seen my signals. He must have seen them, but
he never acknowledged them. There wasn't even a light
showing at Camlet. And I didn't know the island was
tidal. It may sound daft, but I didn't. As it was, he just
waited for the ebb and came over. But if I'd decided to
swim when I'd got nowhere with my signals, as I nearly
did, I'd have been drowned by then. That's if the passage
is as dangerous as you say it is."

She said, "It is, Peter, really. The tide just takes you
right through and out to sea on the other side. You
haven't a hope of getting ashore." But she said it as if her
mind was on something else, and she was not really looking at me. I looked at her and waited. Then she said,
"When did you signal, then? And how? He didn't mention it to me. But then he never mentions anything to do
with the island. It's a sort of total taboo between us. And
of course I never ask."

"At dusk," I said. "The light was going very fast, but I
could have been seen. Well, I must have been. I made a

flag out of the foresail and waved it. I hadn't got any sort of a light."

She said, "But—" Then she stopped and thought. "But I didn't think he was there. Or not till it was nearly dark. He'd been over to Carnholm, doing his shopping. I can't remember exactly when he got back. I didn't think he was back until it was nearly dark. Only I can't be certain."

"I was signalling until nearly dark," I said. "He must just have got back in time." I think I said it mainly to settle her mind. For myself, I was not so sure. My mind was already busy with the implications, only I could not pursue them then.

"He must have," she said. But I was not happy about the way she said it either.

She took herself away from me altogether then. Our minds were too busy for our bodies. We were just two worried people, and the physical tension between us had snapped. "I must be going," she said.

I said, "All right, Letty. But for God's sake be careful. And for God's sake keep in touch as and when you can. If you can't phone, write. I mean, whether anything special happens or not. I must know you're still all right."

"I will," she said, "I promise. As and when I can. But don't try to get in touch with me. Not even a letter. Not now."

I said again, "All right, Letty." But it was not all right. It was all as wrong as it could be, only I did not see what I could do about it. I should have to think about that.

We had so nearly kissed when we met, and now she turned and went off along the cliff without even saying good-bye. The truth is, we had got beyond the formalities just as we had got beyond clichés or even ordinary conversation. We shared a common problem and a common threat, and these were the things we had really had in common from the start. The other things we had in common, the many other things I knew we had in common, had made themselves gradually apparent in the backs of our minds, but we had no attention to give them. Some day I promised myself I should hear Letty Barlow laugh, but at the moment all I had had from her was a bitter smile at the vulgarity of her own affections. With that voice of hers, I knew that the laugh, when it came, would be a miracle, but we had nothing to laugh at yet.

As I went up the slope, I felt that the wind was freshening, though still from the west. If it blew much harder, the boat would be of no use to me, but so long as the wind stayed westerly, she was safe where she was, and I did not have to worry about her. The mooring was under the high west side of the bay, and in these conditions she rode peacefully in the wind shadow while the shallow waters rolled and broke off shore, and on the far side of the bay the black rocks stood up out of a smother of foam. The wind had blown the drizzle away, and my mackintosh flapped itself dry about my legs as I walked up to the car. When I got to it, I took off my mackintosh and gumboots, and put on leather shoes, and took my working papers out of the back seat. I had a new customer to see in the afternoon, and I did not think he would be as easy as Mr. McConnell. I put my thoughts of Camlet away with the boots and mackintosh, and realised, as I did so, how lucky I was. Letty was going back to Camlet, and had nothing else to think about.

It was not until I was home and settled for the evening that I could let myself think about Camlet at all. I say settled for the evening, because for the first time at that end of the year I behaved as if it was winter, lighting the lamps and drawing the curtains after tea, and consciously shutting out the grey, blustery evening outside. The fact that I had a boat still on her moorings in Vance Bay went a bit oddly with this frame of mind, but that did not worry me. As I have said, she was all right in these conditions, and in the back of my mind I had already begun to think that I had one more use for her before I got her in for the winter.

I had two things to think about, a question of fact and a course of action. On the question of fact I knew I could come to no complete conclusion, but the different bits of the jig-saw seemed to fit only one way, even if I could not yet see the whole picture. I thought of things I had seen, and things that had happened, and things that had been said, and things that had not been said, above all the things that had not been said, the silences when I had expected some explanation or at least some comment. I went back over my own earlier assumptions—I had had to make so many assumptions—and found how shaky some of them looked when I came to reconsider them now. I thought I knew more or less what was going on and what Barlow's obsession with the island was. What the explanation of it was I had no idea, but that could wait.

As to my course of action, I believe I had decided on it in an ill-defined way the moment I had left Letty on Maulness Point that morning, perhaps even while I was still there talking to her. I knew what I had to do. What I had to decide was how to do it. What I had to do was to blow the mystery of the island sky-high, and Barlow's obsession with it. It was the mystery and the obsession that were making Letty's life intolerable, and they must be ended. But I must do it in a way which did not involve her, and for which she could not be held responsible. I must tackle Barlow on his own ground, and that meant the island. To say I shrank from the prospect is to understate my feelings. I was afraid of Barlow, simply as a person, and the island itself scared the wits out of me. I told myself that my fear was not altogether rational. I was not sure it would really come to physical violence, and in case it did, I could go prepared, and with any luck look after myself. If the worse came to the worst, I might run away and still get what I wanted. What I wanted was positive knowledge, and I might get that even without an actual confrontation. The trouble was that I was not sure it was physical violence I was afraid of.

As to the way of doing it, there was only one way. There were two ways to the island, by sea and by land, and the land way lay through Camlet. That was where Letty was, and that was therefore barred to me. It was the sea way I must take. I could not take it with the weather as it was, but as soon as it abated, and the tides were right, I must sail to the island. That might be a few days yet, and in the meantime I could settle the details.

So I had my course of action, and much as I disliked it, I felt the easier for having it. The fact that it totally miscarried was, in the event, neither here nor there. Like most determined human actions, it at least produced results. The results were largely unanticipated, but that is the way with most human actions, too.

Chapter Twelve

It was still dark when I got down to the moorings. It should not have been at that time of the morning, even in early October. I knew that the sky must be still heavily overcast, as it had been ever since I had met Letty Barlow on Maulness Point. Daylight would come grudgingly, and when the sun rose I should not see it. The wind still blew from the south-west, a brisk sailing breeze, but steady. I had waited three days for it to lose its gusty violence, and at some time during the night it had. I could only hope it would not die out altogether. I thought it might late in the day, but not before I had to be back on my moorings. The tide had turned an hour earlier, and the boat was just afloat. I could see her from the beach, a dark shape, rocking gently on barely a foot of water. I reckoned I could sail her off the moorings on a starboard reach and let the centre-plate down as soon as I had enough water under me. I had made myself eat and drink before I left home, but I felt hollow with apprehension. I wore gumboots to get the pram off the beach. I could leave them in the pram on the moorings, but I wanted to start with dry feet. To talk of having cold feet may be only a figure of speech, but it rests on physical fact. I know from experience that to sail with wet feet does not help your morale, and my morale was low enough without that.

As soon as I got down to the water, I began to see more. There is always more light on the water than there is on the land, because whatever light comes from the sky is reflected back at you and not absorbed. The water had just reached the bottom of the beach when I carried the pram down to it, stepping gingerly in my slippery boots among the big slimy pebbles and small spikes of seaweedy rock. To turn an ankle at the outset would not help any more than starting with wet feet. If all this sounds very pusillanimous, I can only repeat that I was a cautious sailor, with a very healthy respect for the sea, and I had never sailed before in anything but full daylight.

I had no difficulty getting the sails up. I could see the general shape of things, and my hands knew the gear by heart. It was only the few small droppable things, like a shackle pin or the gudgeon pin of the tiller, that I handled with exaggerated care. The boat rocked gently all the time on the small waves that rolled in over the mud on their way to the beach, and when I got the foresail up, it flapped unnervingly on its loose sheets. There is always this feeling, when you have sail up and the boat still on her moorings, that the wind is much stronger than it really is. It is only when you let the moorings go and sheet in that the thing suddenly takes on a proper proportion. Then the boat becomes a creature moving between its proper elements, and the wind is no longer a noisy menace, but the vital force you needed to bring the boat alive.

When I had done all I had to do and looked round me, I knew that the darkness was already less deep. I could see the shore as a bank of solid gloom above the paler water. I could still see no detail, but I did not need to. All I needed was to know where it was. I planned to sail a long straight leg south-eastwards across the wind, and then, when I was well out to sea, turn and run with the wind under my port quarter. By then I should have as much daylight as I was going to get, and could see where I was going. There would be more sea outside, especially until the tide made and the water got deeper, but I did not think it would be anything the boat could not take in her stride. If I had been on a west-facing coast, there would have been a swell still running from the last few days of wind, but in these shallow waters the sea goes up and down almost with the wind. I looked round the boat, found everything in order as far as I could see it, sheeted the foresail half in and went forward to cast off the mooring. By the time I had got back to the tiller and main sheet, we were already clear of the pram, and as soon as I got her head round and sheeted in the mainsail, we were moving. After a bit I let the centre-plate down and settled down to steer.

I felt easier now. There was nothing but open water ahead of me, and although it was still dark water, it was getting lighter all the time. All I had to do was sail steadily across the wind until full daylight came. Unless the sea was a lot worse than I thought probable, I had, so far as the boat was concerned, nothing to worry about. What lay ahead of me I had no idea, but I had made my plans and could only go ahead with them. The one point of uncertainty was my return journey, because then I should have a deadline to meet. I had to get back to the moorings while there was still enough water to moor the boat and get the pram ashore. And I should be sailing very largely into the wind. If the wind freshened, it might be a very wet and strenuous trip. If it fell light, it might be a very slow one. Obviously a lot depended on how long I spent on the island when I got there. But I had set myself a time by which I must in any event be off it, and I thought that all I had to do was make sure I kept to it. In view of what actually happened, all this planning and calculation seems a little silly now, but it was perfectly sensible at the time. During those last few dark, windy days, and now out here on the dark water, I knew in detail what I had to do, and told myself that my fear was irrational. In the event, I did practically nothing of what I had planned and got horribly frightened doing it. The fact remains that I got what I went for.

Out in the mouth of the bay the full force of the wind found us, but it was still no more than a good sailing breeze with no vice in it. The old boat lay comfortably over on her side and fairly thrashed through the water. On a sunlit afternoon it would have been marvellously exhilarating, and even in these conditions I found time to think, as I had thought often enough before, that a fore-and-aft rigged boat is one of mankind's supreme inventions. I could see a lot more now, but there was nothing much to see except rolling water and grey sky, both moving steadily on parallel lines before the unending current of air. Only the boat, with a human brain in its design and a human hand on the tiller, defied the general order of things and held obstinately across the wind towards the south-east. All along to the north of us the land lay dark and fixed under the grey moving sky. South of us, a long way south by my standards, lay the English coast, but it had not shown up yet. It was the land to the north of us I watched, waiting for it to take shape enough to tell me how far I had come and when I could think of turning in again towards it.

It happened very suddenly and it seemed all in one piece. At one moment I could see only where the land was and the dark shape of its skyline. Then I turned to

119

check the wind direction in the tell-tales, and a moment later, when I looked at the land again, the whole picture had developed detail and depth, as photographic prints used to do when as a boy I had mucked about in a converted airing cupboard in the glow of a red lamp. It was the depth that was important. Unless there is something very conspicuous about it, you do not, by daylight, notice the skyline of the land much, and from out at sea the bottom of the land, where it lies on the water, is the straightest line in the world. What you look at is the ins and outs, the headlands reaching out to you and the bays and inlets falling back between them. This is the shape of the coast as you know it from the map, and until you can see this, unless you are in very familiar waters, you do not really know where you are. The first time I had sailed this way, I could see all there was to see, but I had not had the shape of the coast in my head. This last time I knew well enough the shapes to look for, but up to now I had not been able to see them. Now suddenly there they were, and I knew that on this leg I had come far enough. I must turn almost on to the wind now, but with enough north in my line to take the wind on the other side of the mainsail. I did not want to gybe, even in this sort of breeze, so I shortened sail and turned as near into the wind as the boat would go, went about on to a port tack and then, with the wind on the right side of the sail, turned on to the wind, let out the main sheet and settled down to what I hoped would be a straight run in to the south side of the island.

As always when you turn on to the wind, there was a sudden silence and the feeling that the boat had lost all motion. The silence is real enough, because you are going with the sea instead of forcing your way through it, and the boat goes much more quietly. The loss of motion is pure illusion, because in fact you are going much faster than you were before. Relative to the moving pattern of the water round you, you are moving hardly at all, but if you look astern, you see your wake streaming out behind you in a very reassuring way. I let the foresail out, so that it could catch as much of the wind as the mainsail left to it, pulled the centre-plate up and moved back almost into the sternsheets to lift the boat's head as much as possible. After that there was nothing to do but sit there in the grey silence and point the boat so that the wind did not get under the lee of the sail.

When I first picked out the island, it was in fact dead ahead. I was pleased with my enormously simple piece of navigation, but more than that I was pleased because I was, even from here, coming in to the island from exactly the right angle. It was the right angle because I was from now on out of sight from Camlet. The morning was still a dark one, but to anyone on land my moving sail would be very noticeable, the more so because at this time and at this season no one would expect a small boat to be out at all. For the second time I imagined Barlow in one of his top windows, giving the sea a morning sweep with no doubt very powerful glasses. The first time it had been pure imagination, but Barlow himself had confirmed it. At the time I thought he was lying, but now I was not so sure.

Now that I need no longer worry about getting to the island, I came suddenly face to face with the prospect of going ashore on it when I got there, and it was a prospect I liked no better for being immediately committed to it. I even shrank from it at a merely physical level, because my plan involved swimming ashore, and although I was dressed warm and still had dry feet, I did not feel I had much body heat to spare, and the dark water under that

121

dark sky looked extraordinarily uninviting. The swimming was unavoidable, because there was nowhere to get the boat in safely, still less with any hope of getting her off again in a hurry. I did not know whether I should be in a hurry, but I felt sure that if I was, there would be good reason for it. A man prepared to swim can get off an island at a moment's notice and wherever he can get to the water. Getting a heavy boat off a beach and sailing is a very different matter. I had considered warping her out, as I had that first time under Barlow's instructions, but even that was a slow business, and with the tide still making it would be very difficult to get the distance right. So there seemed nothing for it but to anchor at a reasonable distance off shore and swim in. I had come prepared for it, but I still did not like the idea of it. This had its advantages, because my simple physical apprehension blanketed my necessarily imaginary apprehension of what might happen when I got ashore.

I was coming in very fast now, and still on the right line, so that the dark hump of the island stood up between me and Camlet and even, for the matter of that, between me and the house on the island itself. I should have liked to come in more slowly, but it is very difficult to lose way when you are running before the wind, unless you get the mainsail down and run on the foresail alone. It is easy to spill air out of the foresail, but once the boom is well out, the mainsail holds the air like a scoop, and there is no way to get the wind out of it except to bring the boat right round into the wind. This of course was what I had to do when the moment arrived. The difficulty was to choose the right moment. I sat there, with my eyes fixed on the rocks ahead, trying all the time to judge the distance between us. If I turned too soon, it would be safe enough but would mean a longer swim. If I turned too late, it might leave the boat uncomfortably close to the rocks by the time I had paid out the full length of the anchor warp. In the event I turned a little before I need have done, but it is better to be safe than sorry.

I put the tiller over hard and the boat came round in a surging rush, heeled for a moment as the wind came full abeam and then came right up into the wind with everything flapping. I left tiller and main sheet and ran forward to the bows, where I had left the anchor ready with the warp coiled cleanly on the floor boards. I heaved it over and let the warp run out through my hand until there was enough out to hold her. Then I put it through the fairlead at the stem, held it with a turn round the back of my hand and turned to look at the shore.

I had not done badly, but there was still quite a lot of water between me and the small flurry of foam where the sea broke among the rocks. I watched it steadily for a couple of minutes to see if there was any sign of the anchor dragging, but there was none. The distance did not lessen. The boat swung slightly in the seaway and the sails still flapped in the wind, but she was held all right. I paid out several more fathoms of line, because for a firm anchorage you can never have too much, and because every fathom of line meant six feet less of cold water to swim in. Then I made it fast and got the mainsail down. I bundled it along the boom down the centre of the boat and put a light tie on it to keep it in order. I put a quick-release knot on the tie and made the halyard fast with a single hitch to the belaying pin at the foot of the mast. When I came to get sail up again, it need not take me more than a few seconds. I left the foresail up. It flapped on its loose sheets, but added little or nothing to the wind pressure on the boat. Then I turned and looked at the shore again. We still had not moved. I had done all

I could for the boat. I had nothing to do now but get into that damned water.

I set about it with a sort of desperate determination, because I was working against time anyway, and my only hope was not to hesitate. I took off my wind-cheater and life-jacket and bundled them down in the sternsheets, which is always the driest part of the boat. Then I took off my sweater, trousers and ropesoles and stuffed them into the strong polythene bag I had brought with me. There were two things already in the bag. One was a towel. The other was an old-fashioned life-preserver, which had once belonged to my father. It still had the original thong on the handle. I had carried it several times before in my life but never yet had to use it. I twisted the neck of the bag tight and tied it with a con-strictor knot in the middle of a yard of light cord. The two ends of the cord I tied together in a loop. Then I took off the rest of my clothes, put them with the wind-cheater and life-jacket and stood up in the swimming trunks I was already wearing under them. The trunks were not, in the circumstances, a concession to decency but a safeguard. I had to come ashore on rocks in a mildly breaking sea, and it is easy enough to damage yourself doing that without leaving your vitals exposed. I put the polythene bag on one end of the centre thwart, balanced myself for a moment on the gunwale and then let myself down feet-first into the water.

The shock was no worse than I had anticipated. It had been a fine summer, and the water would not start to get really cold for another couple of months yet. Swimming at Christmas sounds silly, but in an average year the water is not nearly as cold then as it is in May, when the sun may be hot on the beach. When I had got my breath back, I reached up for the bag. I put the loop of cord over one arm and took it up to the shoulder, so that the bag would float over my back as I swam. Then I let go of the gunwale, kicked myself clear of the boat, put my face down into the water and started to swim ashore.

Oddly enough, the exercise did me good. Sailing a boat is in some ways a strenuous business, but it does not do much for your circulation. I had no trouble with the rocks. You have got to know how to do it, but I had come ashore on rocks out of much bigger seas than this. I clambered out over the seaweed and limpets which the sea had not yet reached and made my way carefully on bare feet up the dry shelving rock above high-water mark. When I came to the patches of thrift and coarse grass where the turf still kept its hold, I stood with my bag of clothes over my shoulder and my head just under the top of the sea-bank, wondering what to do. What I wanted was somewhere out of the wind where I could get myself really dry before I put my clothes on. I remembered my original beach, which would be only a little east of where I stood, and thought I would walk across to it on the turf rather than picking my way along the rocks. I scrambled up on to the top of the bank, just as I was in my swimming trunks with my bag on my shoulder, and saw Barlow standing on the turf slope not fifteen yards from me.

He was standing quite still with his back to me, looking up at the skyline above him. He was dressed as I had seen him before, in a black roll-necked sweater, dark trousers and gumboots. He looked immensely tall, standing like that on the slope above me, and the grey clouds moving continuously behind his head only emphasised his total immobility. It was more like a standing stone than a man. The wind blew cold on my wet back, and I felt breathless and naked and utterly at a loss. My one idea was to get down under the sea-bank before he saw me, but before I could move a muscle, he turned where he stood, quite slowly and deliberately, and looked at me.

It was not Barlow at all. The likeness was obvious, but it was not Barlow. Apart from anything else, he was bigger. Barlow was big enough, but this man was enormous. The face was square like Barlow's, but under the cropped grizzled hair the skin was completely white, standing out in the grey light with the startling, unnatural whiteness of a mushroom in dark grass. The hands which hung limp at his sides were white, too. He looked as if the sun never got at him, and the effect was totally repellent. For a moment or two we stood there looking at each other, and then the great face suddenly split wide open in a smile that showed two rows of huge teeth. The teeth were darker than the surrounding skin. It was as if a skull had suddenly grinned at me. He said, "What are you doing here?" The words were Barlow's, and the voice was like his, or even deeper, but this time the menace was unmistakable, like a large animal growling far back in its throat. He was still smiling at me.

My one wish was to get away from him at all costs. It was not only physical fear, but something I had never felt before, a direct apprehension of dreadful evil. I half turned, never taking my eyes off his, and took the one step that separated me from the edge of the turf bank. I moved very slowly, exactly as you do in face of a threatening animal. He moved then, too. He started to walk, almost equally slowly, down the slope towards me. He said, "Come here, I want to talk to you."

My feet were still bare, but I went down the bank and over the rocks below as if I had been wearing climbing boots. The dark water, which I had dreaded when I was in the boat, looked almost desperately far away now. It was the water I wanted, because the water was safe and

above all clean. I slithered and stumbled over the seaweed and threw myself flat into it, and above the splash I
made and the noise of the water among the rocks I heard
behind me a great bellow of derisive laughter. I was past
caring for his contempt. I swam desperately for the boat,
fighting for breath, not so much because of the water
round my head as from the overwhelming fear that
gripped me.

I got a hand on the gunwale at last, and took the useless bag off my shoulder and slung it on board. Getting on
to a boat out of the sea is never easy, because the boat
sucks your legs under it, and the fact that the boat was
swinging and pitching on its cable made it worse, but I
managed it somehow. I rolled almost head-first into the
bottom of the boat, and then knelt on the floor boards
and for the first time looked back.

He was no longer there. The black rocks stretched all
along above the breaking sea, and above them the dark
green slope went up to the dark grey sky, but the whole
place was empty. I had to fight myself not to get sail up
as I was, but I was not mad enough for that. I dried myself with tremendous care, so as to leave no damp skin
under my clothes, and dressed myself as fast as I could.
It was only then that I set about getting under way.

Chapter Thirteen

From this point onwards I was obsessed with time. I did not know what was going to happen, but I knew that something was, and I thought it would happen at the evening ebb, because that was when Barlow would next go to the island. I had to assume that when he did, he would hear of my visit. I must be at Camlet before he did hear of it, or at least before he came back from the island, and above all I must talk to Letty. And here I was a long way from my moorings, and with the wind against me, and until I got to my moorings, I could not get to my car. I am not a racing sailor. I had sailed often enough to beat the tide, but never to gain every possible minute, and now every minute counted.

At least the wind held steady and I could see where I was going. To begin with at any rate there was nothing for it but to sail out to sea on a starboard tack, keeping as near the wind as I could, but without sacrificing too much speed to direction. There is always this problem when you are sailing against the wind, especially in a not very weatherly boat. If you point as nearly as possible where you want to go, the boat will not make much speed through the water. If you hold her more off the wind, she will go faster, but not so much in the direction you want.

It is a perpetual balancing of advantages, and I had not the sort of experience to enable me to make a very accurate judgment. On the face of it, so long as the wind held, I thought I had time in hand. After all, I had set myself in any case to be back on my moorings before low water, and I had reckoned to be some time on the island before I started for home. As it was, I had spent only minutes on the island, but now I had to get over to Camlet in the car before low water, and if possible before the causeway was clear. As always, I had to know where Barlow was. What I really wanted was to see him set out across the causeway before I went to the house. If I made fast time back to the moorings, I thought I could do this, but there was precious little time to spare.

In fact I think I tacked too soon, as your less than expert sailor always tends to do, and I found myself heading inshore again with no hope at all of making it into Vance Bay. I held it for a short time, and then went back again on to a starboard tack. This set the pattern for the first leg of the journey, which was made up of a series of long starboard tacks, as near the wind as the boat would sail reasonably fast, with occasional short jinks on to a port tack to avoid getting too far out to sea. By the time I at last opened the bay, I had got my sailing angles well set in my head, and I held on grimly across the mouth of the bay, so that when I did finally turn in, I could make it to my moorings on the western shore in one long reach across the wind, very much on the line I had taken out of the bay before daylight. This was the more necessary because by now the tide would be running fairly strongly against me. Twice I nearly went about, but held on into the wind more out of obstinacy than from any nice calculation. Then at last I felt I need not argue the thing any longer, and I put the boat about, let out the sheets a little, pointed full across the wind and settled down on to the long port reach which I hoped would take me straight on to my moorings.

I was very tired now, and quite abominably cold. I had been sailing almost continuously since before daylight, and my only break had been a cold swim and the fright of a lifetime. I had some food and a flask of tea on board, but I was concentrating too desperately on sailing the boat to let myself get at it. Once I was ashore and in the car, I should know more clearly how I stood on time, though there was still a lot to be decided about the Camlet end of the journey. For the moment there was nothing for it but to keep on sailing. All the same, the old boat was at her best across the wind, and as she sliced through the grey, rolling sea, I felt an increasing confidence that did something to off-set my physical wretchedness.

The boat at least finished in fine style. Wind and sea both fell away as we came in under the high western shore, but we lost little or no speed until we were round the small wooded point that stood out just south of the moorings. Then suddenly there was the pram, looking, as it always did, very small and lonely as it rocked gently on the dark water under the dark shore. For the last time that year, I turned almost into the off-shore wind, spilled the air out of the sails to lose way and then, at the last moment, let everything go and ran forward to grab the pram as we came alongside it. There is always satisfaction in that moment, and now there was a huge surge of relief as well. For the first time since I had left the island, I pushed the elastic cuff of my wind-cheater back and looked at my watch. There was more than two hours to low water, and I reckoned I had the situation in hand.

All the same, there was work to be done, and done quickly. I got the boat moored and the sails down and stowed, and made everything fast on board. It is a routine operation, but it is one which you generally do in a relaxed frame of mind after a successful sail, and now I was doing everything against time. I skimped nothing that had to be done, because a boat's safety on her moorings depends entirely on what you do before you leave her, but I did nothing unnecessary. Even when I was in the pram, I rowed for the beach as if I was in a racing scull instead of a blunt-ended, clinker-built cockle-shell. By the time I had carried the pram and gear up the beach and got myself into the car, I was short of breath and conscious for the first time of real physical exhaustion. All I had to do now was sit in the car and drive it, but I had enough sense to know that it was no good setting off in that state. It would be no help to Letty Barlow if I piled myself up the bank at the first bend in the lane. I opened my haversack of food and gave myself three minutes by my watch to eat and drink, and for all my mental agitation the tea and sandwiches went down like champagne and smoked salmon, and no doubt did me far more good. Then I settled myself in the driving seat, started the car, turned the heater full on and set out for Camlet.

To a man who does as much driving as I did, driving a car is so much a matter of instinct that he can do it perfectly efficiently, even in a state of fair physical exhaustion, so long as he puts other things out of his mind and has not clogged his reactions with alcohol. I did the drive as fast as I could do it with safety, ignoring speed limits except in the few built-up stretches, but by the end I was in far better physical shape than when I had started. Even mentally I was better off, because I had let myself think of nothing but the driving. It was only when I got into the western end of the loop road that I turned my mind deliberately to what lay ahead, and even then my only immediate problem was what to do with the car. I had to face the fact that Barlow might have been out, at Carnholm or elsewhere, and might be returning to Camlet only just in time to catch the ebb. It was even conceivable that we might find ourselves on the Camlet spur at the same time, but this was a risk I simply had to take. All I could do was to ensure that, if he came along it after me, he did not see my car, which he now had every reason to know by sight. My previous parking place behind the field wall was not good enough. On the other hand, I could not afford to leave it too far from the house, or I should lose precious time finishing the journey on foot. I thought there must be a gate somewhere giving access to the belt of woodlands near the house. I did not know, because on my earlier visit I had done the last bit through the trees and not on the road, but I decided that I had to gamble on it. As a last resort, I should have to gamble on Barlow's being already at Camlet. I had to gamble anyway, and it was better to gamble on the best solution.

In the event, my gamble worked. In the ultimate event, it was unnecessary, but I could not know that, and for the moment it worked. I drove on as fast as I dared down the last slope and then, when I came to the woods, slowed down and looked desperately for my expected gate. Just when I was beginning to lose hope, I found it. It was on the left, not even a gate, simply an opening in the wall with a small overgrown track leading into the trees. There had probably been a gate, but with the woodlands as neglected as they were, it had not been maintained. I slowed to a crawl, turned in through the gap and bumped off into the trees with the weeds and tangled grass swishing and scraping at the sides and bottom of the car. The track went off the road at a sharp angle, and after I had gone about twenty yards, I stopped, got out and looked back. I could still see the road, but only just. By the same token, anyone on the road could just see the tail of the car, but the chance that anyone driving along the road would notice it seemed remote. It was good enough. The only thing I took out of the car was the life-preserver. I hitched the thong around my belt and let the stick fall down inside my trousers at the right hip. Then I locked the car and set straight off through the woods towards the shoreward end of the causeway.

I was glad now of the physical rest I had had during the drive. My legs and feet were dry and in better shape, and I was even glad of the exercise, which did more for my circulation than the static warmth of the car. I did not hit off my line perfectly, but that did not matter. I saw the thicker tangle ahead which meant the seaward edge of the wood, then grey daylight through the tangle, and then I came out on to the bank above the beach and knew I was in time. I had come too far left, and the dark hump of the island lay a little off to my right. But between me and it there was still an unbroken sheet of water, ruffled by the wind and thick with mud from the barely covered bottom, but still continuous. Wherever Barlow was, he was not yet on the island.

I dodged back into the trees again and went westwards, looking for my blaze on the tree. I went as quietly as I could, because for the first time since I had sailed from the other side of that damned island I was in no hurry, and it was always possible that Barlow was already on the beach, waiting for the ebb to clear the causeway. What I should do if the causeway cleared and he did not come I did not know, but there was no need to worry about that yet. For the matter of that, I assumed that if he did not go to the island, there was no immediate cause to worry at all, because he would not know of my landing there. In this I was wrong, though I did not know that till later. But I felt fairly sure he would go, because the morning ebb was still in near darkness, and he never so far as I knew missed a day. When I came to the blaze, I worked my way carefully forward into the bushes at the top of the bank and lay down to wait. A long wait would be a cold business at that hour of a grey October evening, but I did not think it would be long. The tide was still moving across the causeway from east to west, and I could see now how fast it was moving, even as near low water as this. It was breaking in a continuous cloudy smother on the long spine of harder ground, and even with the water no more than ankle deep it would be difficult going, though a man certain of his line might manage it, especially if he had a good stick to help him. With a foot of water I thought it would be very dangerous indeed. There must be much less than a foot now, though more in the middle of the channel, and I did not like the look of it at all. I lay there and watched it, forgetting everything else for the moment in the nasty fascination of it. I do not know how long it was before I realised that the tide had suddenly stopped flowing westwards. It was still falling, of course, but it had divided, and there was a narrow line of dead water, scummy but almost motionless, between the beach below me and the nearest point of the island. I thought there was still some movement out in the centre of the channel, but it was very slight. It was impossible to tell in that grey light when the line I was watching turned from dead water to wet mud, but presently I knew that it was mud I was looking at. The causeway was just clear now, with the water falling back from it on both sides. I was still looking at it when Barlow's head, startlingly close to me, moved across between me and it.

He moved just across my line of vision and then turned his back to me and went down the beach. I found my mouth dry and felt my heart beating violently in my chest as I raised myself on my cold bed to watch him. I had had no more than a glimpse of his face, and that only sideways, but the look on it was murderous. He stood for a moment at the bottom of the beach, staring out across the long stretch of glistening mud. He was dressed as I had first seen him, in waders and a dark jersey. He carried nothing, and his hands hung motionless at his sides, but even from here I could see that his fists were tightly clenched. He stood with his head slightly lowered. He looked like a man going into a fight, and I was conscious of a feeling of enormous, despicable relief that I had not met him on the island as I had at one stage thought I might. Then he moved. He turned for a moment and looked back along the beach in the direction of the house. Then he turned again and set out across the causeway.

I let him go perhaps a third of the way across in case for any reason he should decide to turn back, but he kept going steadily. There was nothing more to wait for now. I got to my feet, stretched my cramped body and with no further need for silence ran as fast as I could go westward through the wood towards the road. I had no thought in my mind now but to find Letty. The house when I came to it looked extraordinarily dark and cheerless. In this gloom you could have expected to see lights burning inside, but I could see none. I had it in mind to open the door and call from the hall, but when I got my hand on it, I found that the door was locked. For a moment I was nonplussed and conscious suddenly of an enormous apprehension. But prosaic as it was, I tried the obvious thing first. I simply rang the bell and waited. I do not know how long I waited, but it cannot have been very long, because even in my desperate impatience I did not ring a second time. The door opened suddenly, and there was Letty facing me in the dark hall. For a moment we stared at each other, and I saw how pale her face looked in the gloom. Then our arms went out to each other and we were locked in a desperate embrace, half lover-like and half like two frightened children in the dark. All we said was each other's names.

I took one arm from her and swung the door back behind me, so that it closed with a thud and I heard the latch-lock click shut. I knew Barlow had the key, but I felt more secure with the grey evening shut outside. When I put my arm round her again, she put her face up to me and for the first time we kissed. Even the kiss had a touch of desperation in it. Then she moved back from me and for another long moment we stared at each other in the dark hall. She said, "Derek's gone to the island."

"I know," I said. "Rather him than me. Tell me one thing. That knock on the head he got the other day, where was it, in front or behind?"

I think I was whispering, though there was no need for it, and she whispered back. "In front," she said. "Why?"

"He didn't fall," I said. "No one in his senses ever lets himself fall on the front of his head. He'd been hit, and I know who hit him."

Her eyes were very wide open now. "You do?" she said.

I nodded. "His brother," I said. "His elder brother."

Chapter Fourteen

She took me by the hand and led me into the sitting-room. We sat down on the sofa, half turned to face each other. She did not put on any lights. It was not really getting dark outside yet, but the sun would be getting low and the sky was still heavily overcast. She said, "How do you know?"

"I've seen him," I said. "Three times in fact. The first time it was just a glimpse of a head and shoulders, so much a glimpse that I thought afterwards I'd imagined it. That was when I first came ashore on the island. Then I saw him again from out at sea, the whole of him this time, but again not much more than a glimpse through my field-glasses. I thought it was Derek, of course. He looked like him, and in any case I assumed it would be him. Then this morning I met him face to face, only yards away. Even then I thought it was Derek until he turned and faced me. He was dressed like him. When he did turn, the difference was obvious, though of course the likeness is there. He's much bigger, for one thing."

She frowned. "This was this morning?" she said.

"Yes. Very early. I came round in the boat. I was fairly certain by then that there was someone on the island, but I had to make sure."

"What happened? What did you do?"

I smiled at her. "Ran for my life, I'm afraid. Any sensible person would have. He wanted to collar me. It doesn't sound very brave, but you don't know what he looked like."

"You got away in the boat?"

"That's right. And as soon as I got the boat back to Vance, I came straight over here. I had to. He'll tell Derek, you see, and I had to warn you."

She nodded. She was not looking at me now. She just sat there, staring straight in front of her. I said, "Did you know, Letty?"

She faced me again. "I knew there was someone there, of course," she said. "Apart from anything else, Derek had to keep him supplied. And of course Derek knew I knew, but it was never mentioned. Yes, I thought it must be Dick. I didn't see who else it could be."

I thought for a moment. "Look, Letty," I said, "I think it's time you told me the whole story. How long have we got?"

"About an hour," she said. "Perhaps a bit more if Derek cuts it fine."

I said, "He's got an hour. We don't know we have. He could come back any time earlier. And he mustn't find me here, you know that. He knows I'm involved now, but he still doesn't know you are, and there's no reason why he should. That's why I went round by sea. Look, is there anywhere we can keep an eye on the causeway while we talk? From inside the house, I mean."

She said, "Only my bedroom, if you don't mind that. There's Derek's room, but he keeps that locked."

The appalling thing was not so much the fact itself as the fact that she did not seem to see how appalling it was. I suppose she had got used to it and now took it for granted. I did not say so. I said, "I don't mind at all, Letty."

She said, "Come on, then. You're right, of course. We must be sure."

She got up, and I followed her out into the hall and up the stairs. It was a very simply planned house. There was just a long landing meeting the stairs at right angles, with doors on each side. She opened the door on the left towards the back of the house and I followed her in, shutting the door after me. Even if your thoughts are innocent, as mine were then, there is something extraordinarily moving, when you love a woman, about the first sight of her bedroom. And here especially, because she was so much alone in that house, and yet this was the only part of it which was wholly hers. It was very like her, too, elegant, austere and scrupulously tidy. I did not have time to take in the details. We went to the window and stood there, side by side, looking out. You could see the whole picture from up here, the island humped under its curve of cliffs and the huge stretch of sea beyond. The water was well back from the causeway now. The small, grim house stood up opposite us on the shoreward slope of the island, but nothing moved at all.

She got two chairs and put them facing the window, but well back from it. The single, narrow bed was in the far corner, away from the window. I wondered if that was significant. In good weather the view would be wonderful, but I thought it was a view she no longer wanted to see. She said, "Dick is, as you say, Derek's elder brother. Derek adored him as a boy and never really got over it. Dick was the older, and the bigger, and the stronger, and the cleverer. I met him, of course, when we were first married. I never liked him, but I tried not to let Derek see it. He was clever, all right, but a bit of a crackpot and with a big streak of cruelty in him. Well, Derek has that too, but very much less."

I said, "A crackpot he may have been, but he's as mad as a hatter now and about as safe as a rogue elephant. I told you, I just ran at the sight of him."

She looked at me, her face drawn with apprehension. "As bad as that?" she said. "I suppose it's been getting worse, with him out there alone on the island. I suppose that's been Derek's trouble."

"It would be," I said. "He'd be going steadily out of control. Like having a tiger-cub as a pet and then finding you'd got a man-eater in the house. But go on."

"Well," she said, "they both went into the Navy. Anything else was unthinkable. It was that sort of family. Dick was five years senior to Derek and went up very fast, but they went in different directions. Derek was always a sea-going officer. Dick was more an operations man, and finished up in Naval intelligence. I don't think anyone liked Dick much, even then, but he was too good to waste. With Derek it was quite different. Everyone who served under him was a bit afraid of him, but they thought the world of him."

"They would," I said. "He's right in the grand tradition. I've never served in the Navy, but I knew what he was the moment I saw him. He should have been an admiral, like his father."

She looked at me quickly. "You've been doing your homework," she said.

I said, "As a matter of fact, it was done for me, I didn't try to do it for myself. But never mind."

She nodded. "Well, that was how it was," she said, "up to—what?—fifteen years ago, it must be, now. Then Dick suddenly sent in his papers and retired. I didn't know why. I asked Derek, of course, but I don't think he did, then. Dick packed up his affairs and went abroad. He'd never married. And then about six months later I knew things were going wrong. I thought Derek was going out of his mind. He wouldn't tell me much, but I could guess the rest."

"Naval intelligence?" I said, and she nodded.

"That's it," she said. "I told you, I thought he was a crackpot, but I hadn't thought he was that sort of a crackpot. It was totally out of keeping with the whole background. But then with that sort it often is. The old admiral was a bit of a fire-eater, and may have bullied him when he was a boy, or something, and perhaps that was how he took it out. But he was clever, right up to the last, clever enough to know that the end was in sight before it caught up with him. He got out, and sold up, and took his pension, and disappeared. It may have been that that finally put them on to him. Anyway, as I say, six months later all hell broke loose, and by that time no one knew where he was. They never did know. I don't think he went east. He can't have, or he'd never have been allowed to get back."

"And he did get back," I said. "He got back here."

"Yes, but not till much later. At the time it was Derek who suffered. I don't think they could ever have seen him as implicated. He wasn't the type, or even in the right sort of job. But of course he was put through it, and then he came out too. I don't think he was forced out. I think he just couldn't stand it after what had happened. Of course nothing ever came out publicly. They don't advertise these things unless they have to. But it would get round in the service, even if it was only a suspicion, and Derek couldn't stand it and came out. It nearly broke his heart. Well, I think it did break it, really. He's never had a heart since, that I could see. But it was Dick who broke it, his adored Dick."

I said, "Poor Derek. I know there's a mean streak in him, but I've always felt he was not so much a bad man as a good man spoilt."

"He was," she said. "He was a good man when I married him. At any rate, I thought so. But that's a long time ago now. I was very young indeed then, too young."

I said, "Letty—" but I knew that what I was going to say was an irrelevancy. "No," I said, "go on."

"Well, we looked about a bit and then came here. Derek's got some money, apart from his pension. It wasn't too bad at first. It's a lovely place, and we had plenty to do. We even meant to do something with that house on the island. And we went around quite a lot. The locals were friendly."

"I know," I said. "I've met some who remember you. You in particular with admiration. But they said you'd sort of dropped out of things about five years ago. They even thought you must have left the district."

She nodded. "That's right," she said. "We did drop out. And it was five years ago, more or less. It was Derek's doing, our dropping out, I mean. He wouldn't have anyone here, and if you stop asking people, they stop asking you. It's natural enough. But it put paid to the marriage. I had got on with Derek in a sort of way. What there was left of him. But with just the two of us in a place like this, things went from bad to worse. And of course Derek was changing, too. He still is. I told you. I had got to the point of knowing it couldn't go on. And then you lost your rudder and came ashore on that island."

I said, "God bless that rudder. I shall keep it, even when the boat breaks up, and hang it in the hall."

Just for a moment she smiled at me. It was as if we

142

both looked for that moment at a possible happiness, ignoring the huge barrier between us and it. She said, "Dear Peter."

"Anyway," I said, "back to five years ago. What happened?"

"I don't know," she said. "I know now that Dick came back. I didn't know at the time. I mean, he didn't just show up here. He must have got in touch with Derek somehow. I suppose he'd got through his money and was on the run. He couldn't touch his pension, obviously. Derek must have thought of the island as the perfect hiding place. We'd made the house habitable, because we'd thought of letting it. It's got its own electricity and water. But I don't suppose he thought of it as more than a temporary expedient. He must still have been fond of Dick in a way, whatever he'd done. Or perhaps he was still just under his thumb. Anyway, there Dick was, and once he was there, there he stayed, and I suppose Derek couldn't get rid of him. Apart from any affection he still felt for him, there would be his pride, too. He couldn't bear to have Dick taken and the whole thing brought out. It was blackmail in a way. Dick knew his younger brother, and Dick never missed a trick in his life."

"But you knew," I said. "After a bit, anyway."

"Oh yes. I told you. I couldn't help knowing he had someone there. And of course I thought of Dick. But by then I'd got beyond asking Derek anything. It just lay there between us, and all the time Derek was getting more and more difficult to deal with. It became a sort of obsession with him, and the fact that he wouldn't talk about it, even to me, only made it worse."

I said, "He's almost out of his mind, Letty. He's cold sane compared with Dick, but he's not in his right mind, even so. There must be an odd streak in the family. It may have been in the admiral, if he was what you say he was. What appals me is what must have been going on all these years between the two of them. Derek and Dick, I mean. A sort of love-hate relation raised to the nth degree. It doesn't bear thinking about. Not that there'd be any love in it on Dick's side. He's bad, Letty, all bad. He's mad too, but above all he's bad. What he did originally wouldn't have been from any sort of mistaken loyalty, not with a man like that. It would have been pure wickedness. As you say, getting back at somebody. Subconsciously it may have been the admiral, but that's neither here nor there. You've got to take people as you find them, and Dick's bad."

We both sat there in silence for a bit after that, and all the time I was watching the causeway. The stretch of mud was no wider now than it had been when I had first seen it. The tide had gone out, as it does, very quickly over the almost level mud, and now it was coming back equally quickly. It was really starting to get dark now, too.

I said, "How was it that Dick was never seen? He must have gone out sometimes. In fact, I know he did."

"I expect he has been occasionally, but not by anybody that matters. There's nothing on the cliffs but sheep. If there was anyone out with them, Dick could have seen them and kept under cover. But mostly there's no one. And for the matter of that, if any of them had seen him, they would probably have assumed it was Derek. You did."

"I suppose that's it," I said. "The thing was so improbable that no one would think of it, whatever he saw. Lights showing at night might have started people talking, but he wouldn't let them show."

She said, "There'd be no one on the cliffs after dark

anyway. They don't go out to the sheep at night except at lambing, and they bring them in off the cliffs for that."

"Anyway," I said, "someone has seen him now, and at close range, and someone who knows he isn't Derek. And by now Derek will know this. At least, I assume Dick will have told him. What's he going to do about it? What am I going to do? And what are you going to do?" She did not say anything. "Letty," I said, "he's dangerous, he really is. All right, he doesn't know at the moment that you're involved. But he might, somehow. As it is, I imagine he'll come after me. I don't know what he'll have in mind, but he'll have to come now. But I can look after myself, or I hope I can. I might even be able to make him see reason about Dick now that the thing's out in the open between us. It's you I'm worried about. Even apart from Derek, I don't like your being here alone with that raving lunatic just over there on the island. I suppose he could walk off it if he wanted to. He must have seen Derek do it often enough. Isn't it really time you got out, Letty?"

She shook her head. "I can't, Peter. I can't, and in any case it would make things worse, not better. So long as he doesn't know about us, I'm all right. I know him as well as anyone can, and I know that."

I got up. It was nearly dark in the room now. I said, "All right, Letty. I'll go, then. The worst thing I can do to you is to let him have any reason for suspecting I've been here. He may come after me as soon as he gets back, and the least I can do is get ahead of him." I took one last look out of the window. "He's still not on the causeway," I said, "and I can be out of sight long before he gets here, even if he's on his way back now. There's no more need to watch. You do what you would be doing anyhow, and I'll go." I thought for a moment. "Is your car working again?" I said.

"Yes. Yes, he had to do it in the end. But he still doesn't let me go shopping by myself. And I've got no other reason to go out, or none that he'd accept. I think he'd go with me to the dentist's."

I said, "If you decide to go, you can go while he's over there. Only for God's sake don't leave it too late."

"All right," she said, "I promise. But I don't think it will come to that."

We went downstairs then and straight to the front door. It was grey dusk outside, but still not dark. It was only in the house that it was dark. We did not kiss. We just touched hands, and I went off down the drive. I heard her shut the door on the lock behind me.

I went straight across the road and into the wood. I was hollow with hunger but I could not go yet. I went through the trees to the edge of the wood above the beach and stood there, watching that narrowing stretch of mud, and all the time the light was going. The light did not matter. I knew Barlow could cross in the dark if he had to, and it would not be fully dark when the water came over the causeway. It was the water that mattered. I had to see the thing out now.

It seemed endlessly slow. The tide does when you watch it, and now it was climbing the slight ridge of hard ground where the causeway was. I had never quite known, when I had watched the ebb, when the causeway was clear, and now, when I watched the flood, I never quite knew when it was awash. But it was, finally, because I saw the ripple where the tide started to flow over it, first in the middle and then right across, moving now from west to east. Even then I went on watching. Barlow was wearing waders, and might still attempt it. But he never came. I could see next to nothing now but the surface of the water, but I should have seen him against it if he had come, and I did not see him.

Even in my desperate anxiety, certainty came at last. I knew then, once for all, that Barlow had not come back from the island, and that if he tried to now, he would never get to the beach. I did not try to think what it meant. I had only the one thing in mind. I went, slowly now, back to the road and up the drive to the front door of the house, and for the second time I rang the bell like any casual caller. The door opened, and Letty was staring at me, her eyes wide with terror. I said, "He hasn't come, Letty. He can't come now."

She came to me where I stood and clung to me. She said, "Don't go, Peter. For God's sake don't leave me now." I moved her back gently into the hall and shut the door behind me.

Chapter Fifteen

The first thing I noticed was that the house smelt of food.
If this sounds a little unheroic, let anyone reproduce, as
near as possible, that day as I had lived it and see what
he feels like at the end of it. I have never forgotten
Homer's sailors, coming ashore after suffering heavy
losses in a nasty encounter. The first thing they do is get
themselves a square meal. Then, and only then, they start
to mourn their dead. Whoever Homer was, he knew
about sailors. I suppose Letty had been getting her husband's supper, but whatever had happened he would not
be home to supper that night. I said, "Letty, I'm very
hungry. Could you find me something?"

She said, "When did you last eat?", exactly as she had
that first time, when Barlow had brought me in off the island. I told her, and she said, "Come on," and took me
along to the kitchen. She did not either fuss over me or
resent my preoccupation with food. She just took me to
the kitchen and fed me. She even made a gesture of eating something herself, to keep me in countenance. It was
not much more than a gesture, but it was a brave one.
When I had eaten, she offered me a drink, but I did not
want one. I could think again now, and I did not want
anything to cloud my thinking. We put the dishes aside

and went back to the sitting-room. It was pitch dark outside now. She put on the standard light and drew the curtains, and we went back to our places on the sofa. We had the house to ourselves for ten hours or so, and I loved her more than I ever had, and thought she loved me, but love takes different shapes in different circumstances.

I said, "Look, two things. First, whatever's happened or whatever's happening, we can do nothing about it until the morning ebb. And second, whatever's happened, I think it must in the long run be to your good. You say yourself the thing couldn't go on. It had to be resolved somehow, and as far as I can see, it could only be resolved between Derek and Dick. If that's what's happening now, so much the better, whatever shape it takes. If either of them suffers in the process, that too can't be helped. If it's Dick, believe me, he's not worth worrying about. If it's Derek—" I broke off with a helpless gesture, because I did not know what to say. She just sat there, looking at me and thinking, as she so often had. I said, "I'm sorry, Letty, but he's no good to you now, and you know it. He's got beyond anything you can do for him. You've got to stop worrying about him some time. It's yourself you've got to worry about. You might even worry a bit about me. I know that's not very noble of me, but I'm pretty heavily involved."

When I stopped, she took her eyes off me and sat staring straight in front of her. Her face was drawn and pale in the lamplight, but quite impassive, and when she spoke, it was almost as if she was speaking to herself, though it was me she was speaking to. She said, "Of course I worry about myself. Anyone does. And I worry about you in exactly the same way and to the same degree as I worry about myself. That's how much you're involved, Peter. I don't worry about Derek like that, not any more." She was silent for a moment, and then turned to me again. I did not move a muscle. I think I almost held my breath. She said, "What do you want me to do?"

"I haven't had time to think about it properly, and I may be wrong. But I think what I'd like you to do is take your car and whatever you want with you, and go now. You needn't go very far. But find yourself a room somewhere, and then telephone me here and tell me where you are. Then just leave me to deal with things here as best I can. At least like that I'd know you were out of harm's way."

"What would you do, then?"

"I don't know. It depends so much what happens. Given a clear morning, it'll be just about light at the ebb, and I must be watching the causeway when it clears. If Derek appears, I'll get out, because he mustn't find me here, and I think he'll come to me anyhow. If it was Dick, I think I'd have to go to the police. If the causeway clears and no one comes, I'll just have to go over. There'll be nothing else for it. We've got to know."

She said, "I don't see how my being away helps. If Derek comes back, it could make a lot of trouble."

"Surely if he hadn't got back in the evening, he'd understand your not wanting to spend the night alone in the house? And I mean—you wouldn't have been with me. I agree, if you said you'd spent the night in a hotel room, he'd check up on it, but he'd find you really had, and by yourself."

She shook her head. "It's not that," she said. "He knows I wouldn't go, not left to myself. And he's suspicious enough as it is." She put out a hand and touched mine as it lay on the sofa. "I'm sorry, Peter," she said, "I can't go. Suppose I went and then heard nothing from you in the morning? I'd go out of my mind. The rest I

150

agree. I don't like it, but I agree. Only if no one comes, and you have to go over, I must be here."

I took her hand and held it in mine. It was very cold, but strong and steady. "All right," I said, "we'll both stay here and both watch the morning ebb. But you must have your car out and ready. If we see Derek coming, you can put the car away before he gets here, and I'll go. If it's Dick, we'll both go. If neither appears, I'll go over and you stay here. But Letty, you mustn't watch, not once I've gone. I don't know what I'd find if I did go, or what I might have to do, but I couldn't have you watching. Just stay in the house. I'll be back as soon as I can."

She said, "All right. But I think Derek will be back. He may simply have left it too late and missed the ebb."

"I don't know what to think," I said. "I don't even know what to hope for. I want an end of it and you clear of it, but how it's to end I don't know."

She took her hand from mine and got up. She said, "I'll go and make up a bed for you. You must be dead tired, and we'll have to be up before daylight." She went out of the room and shut the door behind her. I sat there in the yellow lamplight, conscious of an enormous and growing unease, and wishing Letty Barlow would come back. Once I even got up and went as far as the door to go and look for her, but I knew she would not want that, and went back to the sofa again. The drinks were there on the side table. I almost wished now I had had one, but knew I could neither help myself nor ask for one when Letty came back. Then at last the door opened. She did not come in, but stood there in the hall, looking at me.

"It's ready," she said. "Would you like to go straight up? You need your sleep."

"What about you?" I said.

"I must straighten up in the kitchen. I might not have time in the morning. Then I'll go up."

"Will you sleep?"

"I doubt it, but it's worth trying." She spoke with an almost clinical detachment, like a doctor discussing a nervous patient.

I got up. "Very well," I said. She turned and went up the stairs, and I went after her. It was the same room as I had slept in before. The door was opposite hers. The other door on my side I knew was the bathroom. On her side the other door was Barlow's, but that was locked. She went in ahead of me and looked round. She had put a towel over a chair, and the bed was made up.

"Can you manage?" she said. "I'm afraid you've got nothing to sleep in." She did not offer to lend me any of Barlow's things. She knew I would not use them.

"I'll be all right," I said. I never slept in pyjamas anyway, but I did not say so.

She nodded and turned back to me. I still stood just inside the doorway. I held out my arms to her, and she came into them, and we clung to each other, desperately and without speaking, as we had in the dark hall. Then I moved her a little away from me and looked down into her pale face. I was afraid of the morning, but the morning seemed suddenly a very long way away. I said, "Letty, if you can't sleep, come to me. I don't think I'll sleep much, and if we're neither of us going to sleep, it's no good our being miserable separately."

She put a hand up and just touched my lips with her fingers. "You must sleep," she said. "Try to sleep." Then she took herself away from me and went out and down the stairs. I undressed and put my clothes over a chair. The life-preserver had been on my hip all the evening, because I had had no time to take it off, but now I put it with my clothes. I went along to the bathroom and washed. I cleaned my teeth as well as I could without a brush. There were tooth-brushes there, but I did not know which might be Barlow's. Then I went back to my room and shut the door and got into the cold bed. I pulled the clothes round me, and as I got warmer, a sort of physical drowsiness came over me despite my mental unease. Then I heard a light-switch click on the wall of the passage, and I knew Letty had come upstairs. I did not hear any other sound at all, but after that I could not sleep.

I do not know at what hour of the night it was, but she came to me at last. I think she came for comfort, and because she could not sleep. We found comfort, and much more than comfort. We even found a little sleep. Then all at once the window, which I had left uncurtained, had changed colour, and the morning was on us.

We said nothing, absolutely nothing at all. We both knew what we had to do, and did it. I put on my sailing clothes again. They were all I had, and in any case would do well enough, but I found and put on the pair of gum-boots Barlow had lent me before. I could not shave, because I had nothing to shave with, but I did everything else with a sort of desperate, meticulous haste. I put the life-preserver in my right-hand trouser pocket with the thong hanging ready to my hand. When I went into the kitchen, Letty was dressed and had brewed coffee. There was a tin of biscuits on the table. I could not eat any, but I put a handful in the pocket of my wind-cheater. It was just beginning to get light outside. When we had drunk our coffee, I said, "You go upstairs and watch the cause-way from your window. I'll go along to the wood over the beach. If anyone comes over, you know what we've got to do. If no one comes, even when the causeway's fully clear, I'll go over, and you'll see me go. Then come away from the window, please, and wait in the house till I come back."

She said, "All right, Peter. But if you have to go, come back soon."

I nodded. We did not even touch each other. I went into the hall and let myself out into the grey beginnings of daylight. From what I could see from here, the tide was still over the causeway, but only just. I went through the wood to my tree with the blaze on it. I knew the place well by now, even without the blaze. I went through the scrub to the top of the sea-bank, and found I was just in time. The sky still had its cloud cover, but it was motionless and not too thick. There would be daylight enough presently, but still no sunlight. There was no wind at all. The water lay in a smooth, unruffled sheet between me and the island. Only along the line of the causeway itself a steady ripple showed where the shallow water still moved westwards across it. If there was anyone on the shore of the island, watching the tide as I was watching it, it was still too dark to see him, but the wet mud would reflect the sky almost as much as the water did, and I knew that if anyone came out on to it, I should see him at once. There was no need to hide myself. I just stood among the bushes, watching the water.

I suppose the truth is that I was hoping someone would come, not so much because I dreaded what I had to do if they did not, as because it would take the decision out of my hands. If no one came when the causeway cleared, I had to decide how long to wait before I went over myself, and there were two ways of looking at this. You could argue that if anyone intended to come, there would be nothing, after this long delay, to prevent their coming at once. That would mean that if no one came at once, no one was coming at all, and there was no point in my waiting. Against this, the island was small and bare, and the house either immediately accessible or not accessible at all. Whatever there was to be discovered, to discover it could not take very long once I was on the island, and there was therefore no point in my going over too soon, so long as I gave myself time to get back. I think what I dreaded most was getting well out on the causeway and then seeing Barlow coming to meet me from the other side.

I suppose it was because I was in this state of indecision that the causeway cleared before I was ready for it. I did not see the moment when the ebb ceased to move across it, but suddenly there was the straight smooth line of gleaming mud, and from that moment time began to run, the time in which I had to make my decision and do whatever I had to do. It was much lighter now, still a grey daylight, but daylight nevertheless. The island was no longer a dark outline, and I thought that if anyone came down the slope towards the beach above the causeway, I should see him moving even before he was out on the mud. Anyone out on the mud would be visible in some detail and from some distance, whether it was someone coming from the island or me going to it. The lighter it got, the more I dreaded walking out on to that gleaming expanse. I did not see why anyone should be waiting for me as I was waiting for them, but if anyone was, they could take me as and when they wanted me when I got across. I was sickened at the whole prospect, but still no one came. It was me that was going to have to make the move. The only question was when.

I do not know how long in fact I waited before I finally went. From what happened later, it must have been longer than I thought. I know that twice I started to go down the bank, and twice changed my mind. The third time there was no going back. I went right down the bank on to the beach, but before I set out across the causeway, I did one thing I had already decided on, but could not do until there was no longer any question of concealment. I found a large, almost white stone on the beach and took it back to the bank. I scuffed out a niche for it half way up the brown clay of the bank, and set it there for a mark. I did not know in what circumstances I might have to come back, but I wanted to be sure that when I did, I should have a definite mark to aim at. When I had got the stone in place, I took one more look at the island, saw nothing and set out down the beach and out on to the mud.

There was nothing difficult in the walk itself. The difficulties I had apprehended when I had done it before had been imaginary and deliberately put into my mind by Barlow. But I hated every moment of it. The water was well back on both sides of me now, and I felt extraordinarily conspicuous and defenceless out there in the flat, shining waste. Once I was well clear of the beach, I knew that Letty would have seen me from her window, and I was tempted to turn once and look back at it, but I did not do it. I kept my eyes on the island ahead. After a bit I knew that she would have left the window and gone back into the house. She had promised to do that, and I knew she would. I just kept on walking steadily, watching the near slope of the island for any sign of movement, but seeing nothing. When I got near the beach, I pulled the life-preserver out of my pocket, put the thong over my wrist and turned the stick upwards into the sleeve of my wind-cheater, so that I could have it in my hand at a moment's notice. Once on the beach, I went very slowly, stepping cautiously among the stones and rock in my wet boots and watching every possible cover before I came to it. But still I saw nothing. There was not a sound anywhere except the faint slithering of my boots among the stones underfoot. When I got on to the path, even that stopped, and I walked, for the last time and in total silence, up the slope on to that damned island.

The actual course of my movements I had already decided. There could be no question of my exploring the island, what there was of it, when for all I knew I might be watched from the upper windows of the house. It was the house I had to make for first, and it was the house above all I dreaded going to. It stood there, looking almost black against the dark turf and the grey sky, and stared at me with its blind eyes. All the ground-floor windows were shuttered, as I knew they would be, and the upper windows showed blank white, as if they had curtains drawn inside them. The door was shut. I went carefully round the out-houses, but they were all empty or locked. Then I went back to the door of the house, and turned the handle quietly and pushed, and the door swung open under my hand.

Chapter Sixteen

It was horrible in that house, as if everything had stopped
working, even time. Time had pursued me since the tide
went off the causeway. Urgency and fear, working against
each other, had brought me to this door at this particular
moment, but once inside I felt neither urgency nor fear,
only an indescribable oppression, like a nightmare which
a half waking man tries to shake off, but cannot. I do not
know how much of it was purely physical. Some of it, certainly. There were no identifiable bad smells, and the air
was fit to breathe, but it felt as if it never moved, so that
the faint smell of each particular thing clung close round
it and did not mix with the other smells. The light was
stale, too. There was daylight in the hall now from the
open door, and even when the door was shut, there would
be some from the transom glass over it, but the glass had
been painted over with white paint now turning yellow.
The door on my left was open, and there was an electric
bulb burning in the ceiling, but the light it gave was yellow, too, as if the current was not strong enough. The
door on the other side was shut. The stairs went up ahead
of me. There was more daylight at the top, because the
upstairs windows were not shuttered. It was like looking
up out of the bottom of a well. There was not a sound

158

anywhere, any more than there was outside. The door creaked a little as it opened and then came up against the wall with a faint thud, but after that there was nothing. I stood in the doorway, waiting. In that total silence I thought the noise of the door opening could have been heard all over the house, if there was anyone to hear it. But nothing moved and no one came. I moved at last, but slowly, slowly, like a man in a dream.

The room on my left was a big one, full of stuff, but I did not think there could be anyone in it. I went, stepping very quietly, to the door on my right, and opened it. I had the life-preserver in my hand now. It was a small room, furnished as a kitchen. The only light came from a sort of duct cut into the top of the shutters over the window. It was cut with an upward slant, so that when there was a light in the room, it could not be seen directly from outside. I found later that all the shutters had been treated like this. When the weather was clear outside, you could have seen a small circle of blue sky, but now the sky was grey and did not help much. The kitchen was not quite dirty, and not in any great disorder, but it looked as if everything done in it had been done perfunctorily and then left. There was a little washed crockery stacked in a rack at the side of the sink, but no other crockery about. There were shelves full of tinned food, and an open bin in the corner was full of empty tins. They had been rinsed, but still gave out a faint sour smell.

There was a door in the left-hand wall, and when I opened it, I saw it was a bathroom. There was a bath, a basin and a water-closet, and one towel hanging on a rail. None of it looked very clean, and the air smelt of stale soap and stagnant water. I shut the door, went out of the kitchen into the hall and shut the door of the kitchen quietly behind me. Then I went, still on tip-toe, into the door on the other side.

I caught my breath as I went in, and stood just inside the doorway, looking at it. Here the confusion was indescribable. The room was full of things, so full that there was hardly space to move between them, but nothing seemed related to anything else. It was as if things had been put down where there was room for them, and used for a bit, and then left where they were. The things themselves were the pastimes of an active intelligence, but the whole effect was one of total disorder. There were books put anyhow on improvised shelves, and more books stacked on the floor and wherever there was a level space capable of taking them. If they had been arranged properly, I thought all the books could have gone on to the shelves, but no one had tried to do it. There was a chessboard with pieces set out on it, but when you looked at it, you saw that half the pieces were neither on one square nor another, as if someone had jogged the board squeezing past it in the confusion and never gone back to put the pieces in place and reconsider whatever problem they were involved in. The spare pieces were half on the table and half on the floor under it.

There was an unfinished game of patience on a tray on a chair. I stood and considered it for a bit. Even as the cards lay, there were two cards that could be moved, but no one had bothered to move them. I moved them myself. The cards were almost new, and the dust made a minute friction between my cold fingers and their satiny faces. I was on the point of taking up the pack, but pulled my hand away by a conscious effort of will, like an alcoholic with a bottle. There was even a half-done jig-saw puzzle on a separate table, but the finished part was split zig-zag down the middle. I put it carefully together again, but did not put in any fresh pieces. There was a gramophone, open, with a record still on the turntable and other records, some in sleeves and some not, stacked anyhow round it. I edged my way to it and looked at the record on the turntable. It was Offenbach, which seemed to me only to add to the horror and lethargy of the place.

Then out of the corner of my eye I saw something tall and dark standing half behind the open door, and I swung round to face it, my life-preserver ready in my hand. I did not need the life-preserver, but if I had been a religious man, I believe I should have crossed myself. It was an anthropoid figure, nearly life-size, built up entirely of sea-worn stones from the beach cemented together. It had no features, because the face, so far as it had a face, was made up of one smooth, white stone, but the figure was menacing and unbelievably obscene. It was brilliant work in its way, patient and ingenious and totally wicked. I moved away from it, hardly daring to turn my back on it, but anxious to get the door once more between me and it. As I backed, I caught my heel on a wooden box, which fell over, rattling the things inside it. I do not know what they were. The noise it made was startlingly loud in that breathless house, but still nothing moved upstairs.

I went to the doorway and out of that horrible clutter into the empty hall and the daylight and air from the open door. Despite the two loud noises I had already made, I still moved as quietly as I could, but it was the silence I did not want to disturb. I did not think anyone would hear me, whatever noise I made. Before I went upstairs, I turned and shut the front door. I did not like doing it, but it made sense. I did not think there could be anyone else in the house, and if anyone looked at it from outside, I did not want to advertise the fact that I was.

There was no latch-lock on the door, just an ordinary box-lock with no key in it.

The stairs creaked as I went up them, but I told myself now that this could not matter. There was a window at the head of the stairs facing west. It had some sort of muslin drawn tight over it and tacked to the frame all round. You could just about see through it, but dimly, because the light outside was still grey and the curtain itself thick with dust. All the same, I stood and stared out of it for quite a while. There was nothing to see but the slope of the island and the western curve of cliff that hid Maulness Point, and in between them the silver sheet of breathless water. It was an unbroken sheet as far as I could see from here. If my mind had been working properly, this would have meant something to me, but it did not. I had settled with myself for the fact that the Barlows were not in the house, and I told myself that I must look for them outside. In reality, I think I was just putting off what next I had to do, which was to look into the upstairs rooms. I had no particular reason to want to put it off. I did not think there would be anything to worry me in any of them. It was the sheer superincumbent lethargy of the house itself that seemed to make any action or decision in itself intolerable. Finally I did rouse myself. I took myself away from the window and looked both ways, left and right, along the passage.

As in the house on shore, the passage crossed the head of the stairs and ran the length of the house, but here it was at the back of the house, with windows on one side and doors on the other. There were two doors on my left and one on my right, making two rooms over the big room downstairs and one over the kitchen and bathroom. I turned right and opened the door on that side. It was a square room, with one window facing east and one facing north towards Camlet. The eastern window was obscured like the windows in the passage, but the northern was uncovered. I saw why, and at once knew the explanation of several things which had puzzled me. The only thing in the room was a lamp set on a tripod. It was a signal lamp with a rocker switch behind it and sights like those of a gun on the top. I suppose it was a naval lamp of some sort. When I squinted along the sights, I found them trained exactly through the uncovered window on to the western upper window of Camlet, which was the window of Barlow's locked room. The lamp stood well back in the room, and if the beam was powerful enough, and used in daylight, I supposed it could be seen only where it was meant to be seen. At night the flashing might be seen indirectly from other places on shore, but I did not think it would be used at night, or not more than could be helped. The brothers were, after all, in communication even when Derek was at Camlet. I knew now that that first evening he had never seen my flag-waving at all. It was Dick who had seen me come ashore, and he had signalled Derek, and Derek had come over, even on the night ebb, to investigate. It was all very efficient, and rather frightening, but it did not seem to matter very much now. I went out into the passage, shut the door behind me and went back across the head of the stairs towards the other two doors.

The first room was furnished as a bedroom, but clearly unused. The furniture was adequate, but of that sort of utilitarian quality that people put in holiday houses. There was no carpet on the floor and nothing but a mattress on the bed. The window was obscured like the rest. I took one look round and shut the door and went along to the next. I knew the remaining room must be Dick's bedroom, and it was, and the companion piece to that dreadful living-room downstairs. I opened the door on a faint-lit chaos, and here for the first time the air was palpably foul, so that at first I could not bring myself to go inside, but stood looking at the room through the open door. There were clothes everywhere, no more than could have been put away decently if anyone had bothered to do it, only no one had. They were thrown on the floor and heaped on the furniture in total confusion. I could not see in the dim light whether they were clean, but they did not smell clean. I could just see the bed round to the right of the doorway. It stood clear in the middle of the floor, and was neither made nor unmade. There was a pillow at the head and blankets heaped on the mattress, but I did not think it was ever properly made up, even at night. I took a deep breath of the comparatively innocent air of the passage and went into the room. On my left there was nothing but that wilderness of discarded clothes, but on my right there was floor-space on the far side of the bed, between the bed and the south wall, and when I went closer to the bed, I could see into it. Dick Barlow was, after all, at home, but he had not heard me moving about his house because somebody had beaten his head in.

He lay on his back, with his eyes wide open and staring up at the ceiling. He was dressed only in a singlet and underpants. There was no blood that I could see. He had been sapped with one powerful blow on the front of his head, so that I wondered if he had not been on the bed, and perhaps even asleep, when it had been done. I thought if anyone wanted to kill Dick Barlow without using a gun, to take him sleeping would be the only sensible way of doing it, and I thought Derek had decided to kill him, and that was how he had done it. Only I did not know where Derek was now, and above all else I did not want him to find me here. I backed out of that filthy room, shutting the door after me, and almost ran down the stairs. I tore open the front door and got myself outside. Then I stopped dead. Barlow was coming to meet me, barely ten yards away.

He stopped in his tracks too. I suppose in the nature of things he must have been more surprised than I was. He had a spade in his hand and clay on his waders. It was easy to guess what he had been up to. He looked at me with his eyes wide and his mouth a little open. In that total silence I could hear him breathing harshly in his throat, and his face was the face of the damned. When he spoke, it was in a deep, grating whisper, so low that if there had been any other sound anywhere, I could hardly have heard him. He said, "How did you get here? I haven't seen any boat."

I knew afterwards that I ought not to have answered him. I knew in fact that I had handled the whole exchange wrongly. I should have ignored his question and gone straight on to the attack. I should have told him, what God knows I thought, that his brother was better dead and that he himself had nothing to fear from me. I do not know whether he would have listened, but he might have. I can talk well enough when I believe a thing. But the question was unexpected, and I was not thinking very clearly. There was only one answer I could give. I could not conjure up a boat that was not there. "Oh," I said, "I walked." All my conversations with Barlow had a trick of repeating themselves, only sometimes we changed roles.

He said, "From Camlet?" We had still neither of us moved.

That was where I made my big mistake, but it was one I could not help. To me Camlet was the whole mainland opposite the island. To him, as I realised too late, it meant

165

the house. I said, "Where else?" I even smiled slightly, trying to brave it out.

His mouth shut on that, and his eyes narrowed almost to slits. He said, "Does Letty know you're here?"

This I had to deny, but I have never been a very good liar. I take no credit for this. I am no more truthful than most men, but when I do not believe a thing, I lack the ability to convince anyone else of it. I could not sell so much as a muck-spreader if I did not think it was a good one. I hesitated, only for a split second, but long enough. He said, "I see. So that's it." Then he began coming very slowly towards me.

I still had the life-preserver in my hand, but he had his spade, which was a good deal longer than my life-preserver. I backed slowly in front of him as he advanced. I backed into the open doorway and then, with a quick look over my shoulder, up the two bottom stairs. I reckoned that the narrow staircase and the advantage of height gave me a chance with him when he rushed me, but I had misread his intention. He had more cunning in him than I gave him credit for. He came, still very slowly, into the doorway. The spade was still in his right hand, but I saw his left go into his pocket. I wondered for a moment if he had a gun, but it was not a gun he was feeling for. When he was inside the doorway, he stopped. He said, "You can stay here for a bit. I can come and deal with you this evening. Now I must go and talk to that little wife of mine." He moved then, with astonishing speed for a man of his size. His hand came out of his pocket with a key in it, and he grabbed the door handle and jumped back, swinging the door shut behind him. It shut with a crash, and a moment later I heard the key turn in the lock. I was taken utterly by surprise, and had not moved from where I stood.

But I moved then, and fast. Barlow was on his way back to Camlet, with a murder on his head and more murder in his face, and Letty was at Camlet, waiting for me, because she had wanted to stay, and I had let her. I flung myself at the door, but it was no use. It is not difficult to break a box-lock off a door with a well aimed kick if you are on the far side of the door. If you are on the same side as the lock, you can wrench it off, or simply unscrew it, but that takes time, and I had no time to spare. My only hope was one of the ground-floor windows.

I ran into the cluttered sitting-room and made for the nearest window. The shutters were held in place by the usual iron cross-bar, but for God knows what lunatic reason the bar was held in the socket by a solid steel screw driven into the woodwork. I had no time for niceties. I looked round for the first weapon to hand, and of all things in the world my eyes fell on that obscene figure standing behind the door. I put a foot half way up it and kicked, and it went over, breaking as it fell, with a huge rumble of stones on the dusty floor boards. The stone that made up the head broke off at the cemented neck, and I took it up and attacked the shutter with it, smashing upwards at the socketed end of the bar and the screw that held it. It cannot really have taken very long, but it seemed an age. Then the head of the screw sheared off and the bar swung up with a clang. I wrenched the shutters open in a cloud of dust, and used my stone on the window, striking not only at the glass, but at the glazing bars between the panes. I felt a broken edge of glass cut my hand, but I was past caring. I beat a hole big enough to squeeze through, and squeezed through it, with the broken glass tearing at my clothes.

The grey silence shut in round me after the noisy fury

of my attack on the window, and the air felt chill after the bottled stuffiness of the house. I dropped my stone and ran as fast as my clumsy boots would allow down the path to the beach above the causeway. I was breathing desperately, and almost sobbing as I ran, but when I came to the top of the bank, I stopped, because I knew suddenly that there was nothing more I could do. The water was well over the causeway, running strongly from west to east, and Barlow was about a third of the way across.

Chapter Seventeen

He went with his great shoulders hunched forward, swinging his arms wide to balance himself as he forced his way forward. The water was well above his knees, and where each leg came to rest, the flow swirled round the black rubber wader as a river in spate swirls round the pier of a bridge. I stood and watched him, and if ever I wished a man ill, I wished it to Barlow then. I could see now what the waders were for. Even with much less water than this, gumboots would have been disastrous. I did not think, even so, that he would have gone into the tide at this level if he had been in his right mind. His lunatic rage had driven him on and now he was committed to it. The water was nearly up to his hips now, and he was not yet in the deepest part of the channel.

Once he stopped, with both feet firmly planted, and turned his head for a moment to look back at the island. I do not think he saw me on the bank. I think he was concerned only with the distance between him and the beach. With the better half of my mind I willed him to turn back. If he did come back, I might manage to keep out of his way, and even if I did not, I had more chance with him than Letty had, alone there in that empty house. But he would not do it. He turned to go on, and as he turned, one foot slipped, and his dark arms splashed on the water as he struggled to recover his balance. Then he was moving forward again, but very slowly now, and all the time the water round him was getting deeper.

A few seconds later it happened. One leg went suddenly from under him, and the great dark body canted sideways with the arms flailing at the air and water. Then the other foot lost its hold, and he was down, slashing at the water with his arms, and the next moment the tide had him. It rolled him over sideways and he went eastwards with it, half swimming and half still trying to find his feet on the slippery bottom. Then he was swimming, with only the grey head and the dark arms visible above the grey shining surface, but I knew now that the water would be into his waders. I remember that a fisherman friend of mine once told me that even a salmon river in spate can be a nasty proposition if the fisherman falls and gets his waders full, and Barlow had much more than a salmon river to contend with. All the same, he kept on swimming, but he was going away eastward faster now, and I knew there could be only one end to it.

I could still see his head and arms, but they looked very small now in the wide sweep of grey water. Then for a moment they vanished altogether, but they broke surface again a yard or two further on, and he was still swimming. Then they went under again, and I thought it was the end, but again he came up, only now he was not swimming, but just thrashing at the water with his arms in a desperate effort to keep afloat. When he sank the next time, he sank quite slowly, and I stood there, straining my eyes in the grey light, watching the grey surface of the water, and no longer quite sure where to look for him. I waited for what must have been minutes, but I still saw nothing. That big, menacing body was under the water now, drifting inexorably round the eastern end of the island and out to sea, and where the tortured, angry mind was I did not find it in me to speculate. I turned and went slowly back up the slope towards the house. I knew what I had to do, but I had time to do it. The one thing I hoped was that Letty Barlow had kept her promise and had not been watching from her window. Whatever she felt about her husband now, and whatever he had had it in mind to do if he had got across, what I had seen was not for her to see.

The spade lay on the ground just outside the door. I suppose Barlow had dropped it when he ran down to the causeway. He had known the state of the tide more accurately than I had. He must have known I could break out of the house before very long, but he had known that, even when I did, I could not get off the island. I was there at his pleasure, until he came back for me at the evening ebb. Only he had not judged the state of the tide accurately enough. But I had no use for the spade. I was not going to complete the process that Barlow had set in train. I had a better answer than that, though it was an answer which for understandable reasons was not open to him.

I went up to the door, measured my distance, raised my right leg and kicked with all my force at the face of the door just beside the handle. The door shuddered, but did not give way. The lock was more strongly screwed on than I had expected, but I did not think it could withstand my battering indefinitely. Something had to go, either the lock itself or the socket on the door-frame where the bolt was housed. My rubber boot was not easy to kick in, but it cushioned the shock on my foot, and when I kicked again, I put all the weight I had behind it. At the third kick the door moved in a couple of inches to a sound of splintering woodwork. It was not free yet, but the screws were giving way. I tried my shoulder on it, but only hurt my shoulder. It was the fourth kick that did it. The door burst open in front of me, and I went with it. I finished on my hands and knees almost at the foot of the stairs, and as I crouched there, I heard the lock pull loose from the socket and fall to the floor with a clatter of loose metal. Then the silence of the house closed round me, and in the silence I got slowly to my feet, steeling myself for what I had to do.

I went out of the door again and sat for a minute on the turf, getting my breath back. As I sat there it came to me suddenly that I was very thirsty and probably hungry. I got up and went into the kitchen, and turned on the cold tap over the sink. The water came clear enough, and I drank it eagerly. I drank only from my hands. I could not even bear to use one of the washed cups on the draining board. Then I went outside again and ate the biscuits from the pocket of my wind-cheater. The kitchen was full of food, but that too I could not bring myself to touch. I felt a bit better after that, and in any case I could not put the thing off any longer. I needed the flood tide, and it would not flow indefinitely. I got up and went inside again, and this time I went straight up the stairs.

The air in the bedroom was fouler than ever, so foul that I even thought of getting the window open, but I knew I must not stop for that. I needed a rope, but did not know where to look for one. Instead I found a strong cotton shirt among the jumble of clothes on the floor, and took it and walked round with it to the far side of the bed. I did not look at anything more than I had to. I tied one sleeve of the shirt round each of the great cold ankles. The bed was between me and the door, and I pushed it back to the far side of the room, under the masked window. Then I gathered the body of the shirt and rolled it into a rope, and took the twisted stuff round both hands and threw my weight backwards in the direction of the door. The thing I had to move was immensely heavy, but the floor was bare, smooth boards, and I got it moving at last. I thought of adding another garment to the shirt, so that I could turn and take the improvised rope over my shoulder, but I knew that my only real reason was that I did not want to see what I was dragging after me. You can pull more strongly backwards than you can forwards, because you can pull with your arms as well as your legs. I did not go straight for the door because I was afraid of unspeakable difficulties with the door-frame. Instead, I made straight out into the middle of the room, kicking dirty clothes out from under my feet as I went. Then I turned and made for the door on a course at right angles to the wall. I backed straight through it until I came up against the wall of the passage, and only then I altered course and made for the head of the stairs. There too I made the widest turn I could, and started down the stairs, watching the great inert thing behind me until the near end of it was well over the top of the stairs. I was full of sick panic that it would suddenly take off on its own and come down on top of me, but I had to get it as far as I could. When I had gone as far as I dared, I let go of the shirt and went back up to the top, clinging tight against the banisters to avoid touching anything as long as I could.

When I got to the top, I had no choice. I crouched with my back to the wall of the passage, and put my hands on the shoulders. They felt cold and slightly waxy, like butcher's meat. Then I began to heave forwards. I heaved until gravity took over, and then I knelt with my eyes shut while the thing slithered and bumped down the stairs. The noise it made was the worst noise I have ever heard, but when it stopped, it stopped down in the hall, and at least I did not have to disentangle anything from the banisters. I think it was too heavy to stop once it had started to fall. I opened my eyes and got to my feet and went down the stairs after it. I got it out of the door and on to the turf, and from there on the journey was mercifully all downhill. I had heard somewhere that when they drag the deer carcases in the Highlands, they drag them from the front of the body, but there was a reason for that which did not apply here. I did not know how the weight of a stag compared with the weight of a man, but I could not believe that any deer carcase was as heavy as this was. All the same, the turf, still slightly damp, made easier going than I had expected. It was when I got to the path that I had to go almost foot by foot. I was panting like a runner and sweating under my too warm clothes, but I could not bring myself to stop and take anything off.

The last bit was over the beach, and that was easier, because the pebbles were wet and rolled slightly under the smooth thing sliding over them. In any case, there was not much of it. The tide was well up the beach now. I backed straight into the water, going as far as I could without getting it over the tops of my boots. Then I stopped and did what most of all I feared to do. I untied the shirt from the ankles and took it back on to the beach. Then I took the last two remaining garments off the body. I did not try to take them off in one piece. Whether or not I could have I do not know, but I could not face what would have been involved. Instead I took out my knife and cut them where I had to, and pulled the cut cloth piecemeal from underneath. I put the tattered stuff down with the shirt and knew that the worst was over.

I went to the top of the beach and took off all my

clothes from the waist down. My top clothes I rolled up above the waist and fastened them with my belt to keep them out of the water. I was still so hot that the chilly air came as a relief to my skin, but the water, when I went into it, struck deadly cold. I waded out and took hold of the feet and pulled until the whole body was in the water. Then I got behind it and put my hands on the shoulders again and pushed. I did not mind touching it in the water nearly as much as I had on dry land. Sea-water for me has a sort of intrinsic cleanliness which can exorcise almost anything. The beaches in these parts are mostly narrow and very steep, and it did not take me long to get as far as I could. Then I set my feet firm on the stones and pushed the floating thing out into the sea. It hung for a bit, almost wholly under water, but still afloat, and then the tide took hold of it and it began to drift eastwards. I went out of the water on to the beach, and when I looked round, I could no longer see it. I dried myself as best I could with my handkerchief and put my clothes on again. I was cold now, and the clothes on my upper half stuck clammily to my skin. I picked up the shirt and the torn clothes and walked up the path from the beach to the house, glad to be on the move.

When I got to the house, it was as much as I could do to go into it again, but there were things I had to do. I went straight up the stairs and threw the clothes into the open door of the bedroom. There was so much stuff on the floor already that they did not show. Then I went downstairs and into the living-room. I put the shutters back over the shattered window and dropped the bar into the socket. Then I went out of the front door and pulled it shut behind me. There was no way of fastening it securely, but I held it tight shut and drove a piece of wood under it with the toe of my boot. I thought it would hold

against anything but a strong easterly, and in any case it
was the best I could think of. I was conscious suddenly of
a total and appalling exhaustion, and I could not think
very clearly about anything. I remember having it in
mind at one moment to set fire to that damned house and
burn it down. There was electricity in the house and a
cooking stove of sorts, and there must be some way of
getting fire. But I knew it would not be a reasonable
thing to do. There was nothing physically wrong with the
house that a few hours of hard work would not put right,
and I supposed Letty Barlow would be selling the place
presently. Whatever I felt about it, it was not for me to
destroy her property. There was a great deal wrong with
the house that was not physical, but that could be left to
someone else to discover.

I went slowly down the path and sat down on the turf
at the top of the bank, facing the unseen causeway. I had
another six hours or so to wait, and then I would go back
over it again. For the present I just sat there with my eyes
shut, trying not to think. I could not stop myself thinking,
of course. The thing I thought about most was the story
Barlow had told me when he had taken me back across
the island that first time, his story about the two brothers.
I could not get it out of my head. A ghost story should
have its roots in the past, not in the future. I had been
told a ghost story by a living man who was now himself
one of the ghosts. It did not seem right.

Chapter Eighteen

I must at some point have gone to sleep. I could remember not wanting to sit up any more, and lying back on the turf slope, and I suppose that when I did, physical exhaustion and mental shock put me under. When I woke, I was deadly cold, but the worst of the horror had died out of my mind, and I could think more clearly. The grey day was turning towards a grey evening. The stretch of water in front of me was still unbroken, but it was moving now from east to west. The tide had turned while I slept, and gradually, under the moving water, the causeway was coming to the top again.

I got up and stretched and knew I had to be on the move to get the cold out of my bones. I went back along the path to the more level turf, forcing the pace deliberately. I had not meant to go near the house, but I suddenly remembered the spade, which I had left lying where Barlow had dropped it. I did not want to leave it there. Somewhere on the island there was a freshly dug grave. I did not think there was soil enough for it to be a very deep one, but a grave looks like a grave, however shallow it is, and a used spade left lying made too obvious a connection. I went up the slope to the house and picked it up. I was not going to have anything more to do with

177

the house itself, but I wiped the blade roughly on the turf, and took the spade to one of the unlocked outhouses. I unbolted the door and put it round the corner, leaning against the wall behind the swing of the door. It did not look out of place there, and in any case no one would see it unless they went right inside. I suppose I ought to have found the grave and filled it in, but I had no heart for that. The winter was coming on, and the weather would soon do most of the work for me.

Then I walked back over the island to the beach where I had first landed. I do not know why I went there, but I had to go somewhere, and that was where the whole thing had started. I walked, and at times jog-trotted, over the hump of the island, and when I came to the cleft, I forced my way down the path between the thorn-bushes to the tiny beach. There was quite a lot of it uncovered. The tide must be lower than I thought. I wondered whether perhaps it was a very small neap tide that had been upsetting everybody's calculations. The heights of the tides did not generally concern me as much as their times, and it would not have been a thing I should have in mind. I could not tell the actual time, because my watch had stopped. I did not think the water had got at it. I thought it had stopped because in that grey dawn at Camlet I had forgotten to wind it. I looked round the beach, almost idly, for some evidence of my landing. On an inlet beach like that the driftwood goes up and down with the tide until it is left high and dry or rots down among the stones. Left to itself, it never goes out to sea again. I found nothing likely but a small chip of fresh-cut wood, which I thought must have been a by-product of my work on the rudder. At any rate, I picked it up and put it in my pocket. I did not think I should ever come back to the island, but if I did, it was here I would come ashore. I had to cross the causeway again once more, very soon now, but I thought that when I had done that, I would not go back over it again for all the tea in China. At any rate, it was time I was getting back to it again now. I left the beach and walked back over the island. I was warmer now, and when I came to the bank over the causeway, I knew I had not much longer to wait. Already the ripple was well formed where the ebb passed over the spine of higher ground, and soon the mud would appear and the water cease to flow. For the last time I sat and watched it. It was as dark now as it had been when I had watched it more than twenty-four hours before. The clouds were not so thick, but the ebb was later. I could just see my white stone on the opposite bank, but I was waiting now until I had a clear path to walk on.

It was grey dusk when I went down the beach and set out over the mud, but the line was clear enough, and I walked straight over. Just as I came up on to the beach, a dark figure came out of the bottom of the road by the house and turned in my direction. I could see no detail, but I knew who it was. No one else moved like that. She came on resolutely, making for the end of the causeway. She in her turn had waited from one ebb to another for someone who had not come back, and now she too was coming over to see for herself what had happened. The courage in that slight, determined figure must have been tremendous. If I had still been on the mud, she would have seen me at once, but I was on the beach, and it was the mud she was watching. She must have come on twenty yards before she saw me. For a moment she stopped, peering at me in the gloom, and then she began to run. I ran too. We were both wearing gumboots, and I do not know why we did not break an ankle between us, running across the slope of the dark beach like that. Per-

179

haps love, like drunkenness, has its own built-in safe-guards. At any rate, we met, and clung, and the horror of the past twelve hours drained out of my mind like a bad dream in the morning sunlight.

We did not say anything. We were very good at not saying anything, and quite content with it. We just walked back along the beach, holding hands and going more carefully now, as if we did not want to risk any-thing. But she had to know, and just before we came to the road, she asked her question. She said, "Where's Derek?" I was filled with enormous thankfulness, because I knew then that she had not seen anything.

There was nothing for it but brevity. I said, "He's dead, Letty. They're both dead."

She did not stop walking, but I heard her sharp intake of breath and felt her hand tighten convulsively in mine. "What happened?" she said.

"He tried to get back across the causeway, but left it too late. The tide got him. He was wearing waders. He hadn't a hope."

We walked a few more yards in silence. Then she said, "Poor Derek."

I was determined to make her face it, once for all. I was not going to have the rest of my life haunted by poor Derek. "That's as may be," I said, "but he'd have killed you if he'd got across. That's what he was coming over for. He'd already killed Dick."

She did stop then. She stopped and turned to face me, staring up at me in the dusk with her white face and great dark eyes. "No," she said, "oh, no."

I said, "Yes, Letty, I'm afraid so."

For a moment or two she went on staring at me, but she saw the truth in my face. Then she turned, and we went on walking back to the house. It was not until we were almost there that she said, "Where's Dick, then?"

"He's in the sea, too. I put him there myself. Derek killed him in the house. They're both in the sea. I don't know about the tides round here. If Dick's found, he won't be identified. No one knew he existed, after all. If Derek's found, I suppose he will be."

She saw the problem at once. That was the hard practicality in her mind which I did not find anything but admirable. "What had I better do?" she said.

I said, "I've thought about that. I think you had better report his death now, as if it had happened at the evening flood. You've got over an hour. You can say you saw it happen. That will be the only lie you need tell. The gap of twelve hours doesn't matter."

She did not baulk at this at all. She said, "All right, I'll do that. But you must be gone by then."

I said, "All right," in my turn, because I knew it was the only thing to do. Then I said, "But there's a good deal of clearing up to do. You'll have to let me come over and help you."

"No," she said. "No, Peter. I can handle it on my own, so long as I know I'm on my own."

"There's the island, too," I said. "The house is in a bit of a mess."

"What sort of a mess?"

"No evidence of murder. I didn't mean that. Just the evidence of Dick's occupation. He was living pretty nastily at the end." I thought of the one piece of evidence which I had smashed into a heap of stones behind the living-room door. I had not realised at the time what a good thing I was doing. I did not think there could be anything else in the house as nasty as that.

She said, "I can handle the island, too. I've got a friend

181

who'll come and help me if I need her. But I don't see why I should. I went there often enough in the early days."

We were in the house now. I pulled off Barlow's gumboots and put them back where I had found them, and put my own shoes in their place. Then I went into the kitchen and found her already at the stove. "You must be starving," she said. "You always are, every time you come here." Just for a moment we smiled at each other, very briefly, as if we hardly knew whether we dared smile, or even whether we ought to. "Don't worry," she said, "I like feeding you."

I said, "You're going to get plenty of opportunity," but she did not say anything.

When the food was ready, she said, "Would you like a drink? I think I should."

"We'll both have a drink," I said. "I'll get them." I went into the sitting-room and poured out two moderate whiskies and brought them back into the kitchen. When we had the glasses in our hands, we looked at each other, as uncertain what to say over our drinks as we had been about our smile. In the end she just reached out and touched my glass with hers, and we drank in silence. When the food was ready, we both ate. I did not ask her how long it was since she had eaten. She had probably gone hungry longer than I had.

When we had finished, she said, "Now you must go, Peter. You must go, and I must phone the police. Not quite yet, but presently. Will you be all right? I never asked where your car was."

"It's not far," I said. "I'll be all right. What about you?"

"I'll be all right, too," she said.

I went out into the hall, and she came with me. It was

still dusk outside, but the hall was dark. At the door I said, "When shall I see you again?"

She came up to me and took my hands in hers. "Not for a bit, Peter," she said. "You understand, don't you? I've got a good deal to get over and a good deal to decide."

"I understand," I said. "How long, then, Letty?"

"Give me six months."

"As long as that?"

"I think so, yes. It may be less. You must leave it to me. I'll get in touch with you when I'm ready. But it won't be longer than six months, I promise. You get on with your job. I'll be very busy here for a bit in any case."

"All right, Letty," I said. We kissed once, very gently, and then I went out of the house and started walking back to my car. It looked a bit neglected there among the trees, but it started all right, and I backed it out on to the spur road without damaging anything. I backed it out with its tail to Camlet and its head to the main road. Then I settled down in the seat and started driving.

The house seemed very quiet and rather cold when I got into it, but a few minutes later the phone rang. I ran to it and snatched up the receiver and said, "Yes?" But it was only Mr. McConnell, a little drunk by the sound of him, on about his muck-spreader.